S.J. Klapecki

STATION SIX

BLACK DAWN SERIES

With the Black Dawn series we honor anarchist traditions and follow the great Octavia E. Butler's legacy, Black Dawn seeks to explore themes that do not reinforce dependency on oppressive forces (the state, police, capitalism, elected officials) and will generally express the values of antiracism, feminism, anticolonialism, and anticapitalism. With its natural creation of alternate universes and world-building, speculative fiction acts as a perfect tool for imagining how to bring forth a just and free world. The stories published here center queerness, Blackness, antifascism, and celebrate voices previously disenfranchised, all who are essential in establishing a society in which no one is oppressed or exploited. Welcome, friends, to Black Dawn!

BLACK DAWN SERIES #4

SANINA L. CLARK, SERIES EDITOR

ISBN 9781849354783
E-ISBN 9781849354790
LCCN: 2022935889

AK Press
370 Ryan Ave. #100
Chico, CA 95973
www.akpress.org

AK Press
33 Tower Street
Edinburgh, Scotland EH6 7BN
akuk.com

Cover art by Juan Carlos Barquet, www.jcbarquet.com
Cover design and logo by T. L. Simons, tlsimons.com
Printed in the USA.

To Joan; thank you

STATION
SIX

Chapter One

Some sixty-million miles away from Earth, Max was hungry, nearly broke and standing in line for an ill-advised Everything Burrito. "Everything," of course, still meant there was no meat; only off-brown, tasteless soy protein. But that was the price they paid for not being wealthy enough to go to the proper restaurants. They were still tabulating the money in their head, how they had three days left until payday but needed to eat before work and just didn't have the damn time to make breakfast that morning. Their mind broke their current balance, plus payday, up into portions for rent, bills, HRT, food, and that meager sum just shrank further.

"That'll be seven twenty-three," mumbled the employee through his exhaustion. Poor man didn't even have the time to cock his hat right. Max extended their hand, the corp-mandated pay-pad on the heartline of their palm passing under the laser reader. The machine beeped a merry tune, and Max turned around without saying thanks, hurrying off to work.

A twinge of guilt pulled at them as they considered their bank account shrinking: the debt they had to pay to LMC; the rent they had to pay to Kallihan Housing; a dozen more tiny costs and infractions and hits to whatever they made. In theory, there was a saving's account—one they hadn't checked outside an automated email cheerily informing them that at the current rate, they'd have "enough to retire by 2856! Only 723 years left!"

Fucking joke.

And overhead, as they moved through the food court, was the station owner. Not in person, of course. On the massive screens that flanked each side of the food court there was a blond man with chiseled features, a butt chin and so much product in his hair it looked like a congealed mass of platinum dye in the light. Mr. Ashe, CEO of LMC and personal overseer of this Station Six, was speaking his pre-recorded announcements.

"Hello, my LMC family." Max wished they hadn't broken their earbuds—what they would give for some chance to let electro-drone albums drown out his words. But they supposed the world hadn't been fair thus far and wouldn't start now. "I am pleased to report that because of our hard work, preparations for the future have been going along quite well. The Automated Future Plan is in full swing—all thanks to you. New vistas to explore are opening. New worlds are being made. And you all are vital to that. Remember: LMC leads the future. The future that we all build together. Any concerns about your coming employment opportunities may be directed to the relevant offices."

Max concealed their rage. If they had just an ounce less restraint, an iota less fear, they would throw the burrito at the screen and start ranting. They couldn't, of course. That'd get them arrested, searched, security would get involved. It would be a whole mess. They bit their tongue as they walked.

Seven weeks ago, automation had been announced. Seven

weeks ago, Max felt the floor of the world fall out from under them. The entire station was going to be converted, made into a resort and vacation destination with exactly as few human personnel as it needed to stay functional. Every damn worker was going to be given a new "employment opportunity" elsewhere. Hearing that, reading the words, seeing over and over again the jobs available, struck Max like a harpoon to the heart. Mars. Io. Europa. The Asteroid Fields.

The writing was on the wall. If automation went through, LMC would just send them deeper into the solar system, trap them in another contract, another binding set of legal chains. Everything they had built here, such as it was, would be uprooted again. They had been displaced once, when they signed up for this station. They remembered the recruiter's office clearly. Sterile, clean, eggshell colored and logo filled. The kind smile of the cute recruiter and the scratch of a stylus against a screen. A five-year contract to work on Station Six, followed by a trip back to Earth, provided they could pay off the cost of the trip—monthly installments, of course. It sounded good, what with all their other prospects dissolving after they gave up on college.

Those debts, starting with the cost of a roundtrip and compounded by rent and utilities and more, had done nothing but grow. Not through any fault of their own. Paid eight bucks an hour, they ended up splitting that up best they could, but between food, rent and utilities, it was never enough to fully cover the basics. Every month there was something that had to be shifted, an offer from the company to mercifully take on whatever Max couldn't pay for and add it to that mountain. With interest, of course.

It was a long, long way to work, and they were already pretty late. Or would be. Slept all of ten minutes too late and now they had to cross the football-field-sized expanse of the food hall, after going through the elevators that lead from the apartment's low floors all the way to the connecting point. Moving sidewalks ferried people back and forth—those who had the leisure to not walk. There was no such leisure for them, though. Max's backpack, with a laptop, hard drives and a whole array of tools for accessing computers in variously illegal ways, pulled at their shoulder as they power walked through the crowds.

The station was huge. A city in the stars, as a faded poster on the wall reminded Max. Divided into sectors A to H, each one a small town with chemical, logistical, agricultural, residential, security and medical sections. Max had only ever seen a small slice of the whole station, of even their Sector A. There wasn't much time to explore beyond their apartment, their favorite eateries and their workplace. A workplace that they were now rapidly approaching.

They got their ID ready as they made their way to a security officer—someone who looked less like the rent-a-cops they supposedly were and more like soldiers. Clad entirely in black armor with prominent bulletproof vests and tinted visors, they always looked like they were trying too hard to be threatening. The gun was enough; looking like the worst result from a low-tier loot box was just showing off. Of course, just because they looked overdressed didn't mean Max wanted to antagonize them. So they quietly showed their ID to the officer and made their way to the transit hub.

As they passed through, they saw someone in the hall being searched up and down by a guard. He insisted he had done nothing wrong, but the guard said something about "illegal organizations." Max felt sick as they walked by. A protest against the automation had been broken up a few weeks back with batons and clubs. Someone who had been putting up an unapproved poster was fired, arrested and sent back to Earth with full criminal charges for corporate vandalism and disturbing the peace.

They never felt safe, never felt unwatched. Security guards had come and inspected their apartment, searched through their things before. It was fun to talk shit, call them rent-a-cops, but every time Max passed one, they just hoped they wouldn't be singled out. So far, they hadn't been.

The entire transit hub smelled like ozone. The ionized hulls of docking spaceships leaked particles and bits of dust and everything else into the station every time they touched air. The ground around the docking bays were covered in that thin, gritty film. It wasn't particularly dangerous if you didn't disturb it too much. Cleaning robots were, of course, supposed to come in once a week. Their work was almost always erased by the day after, though. Too many ships, too few robots and a space too big for someone with a broom to clean it all up. With two floors, twenty hubs on each and hourly quotas, nothing could keep the docks clean.

The automatons that had already been delivered sat on the far, far side of the transit hub, where specialists and engineers imported from Earth only a few weeks previously were already hard at work setting them up. The sound of power tools and mechanical assembly rung throughout the mostly empty station. It was one of those between times, when nothing was supposed to be coming in, shifts were changing and people were absolutely bored out of their skulls.

One such bored person was Joseph, waiting for Max outside their shared office (really, more of a cubical with a computer that told them what was coming in and when) with an e-cigarette in his mouth and an annoyed expression on his face. He stood next to the ever-ignored "No Smoking" sign, his bright, orange eyes glinting in the harsh overhead light. Those eyes weren't organic— at least the irises weren't. Some barely thought-out decision to "stand out" years back. Tattoos crossed up and down his olive arms, bright flashes of color in avant-garde patterns that made him look halfway between a living modern art exhibit and an absolute douche.

"Ey, Max, you're a bit late," he said. "But I won't hold it against you. Boss asks, you were here with me."

"Yeah," Max said. "Sure. The cameras will lie, too." They gestured up to the CCTV that watched them all. Insectoid eyes, blinking red to let everyone know they were always observing. Joseph chuckled.

"Sure, they will—they're not dicks, are they? Anyways, kid." Max bristled. They hated being called that, but never got him to stop. Never got him to give up the fact he was two years their senior. "So, when it comes to the meeting with Vic," Joseph chose his words carefully. Max could see his expression shifting as he searched for the right mix of euphemism and directness. "She's available tonight, if you got the time. Turns out she needs a little, ah, tune-up work. Told her you could provide. Does that work out?"

"Yeah, I think so."

"Good. Now," he looked up, suddenly aware of the cameras and their microphones, "we shouldn't talk all too much about it now."

"That works for me."

The unspoken part, of course, was that Vic, or Victoria, was one of the more respected members of the Protection Forces—that particularly illegal organization within the already illegal Federation of Unions that so plagued the station, one that Max every so often was able to scrounge up enough to pay dues to. A bunch of rabble-rousing radicals who wanted more than the bountiful nothing that LMC so kindly charged them for.

Max and Joseph entered their shared office. Inside was a poster urging them to "Keep the Pace!" because they were "Building the Future!" It had been stripped away, with big tears and chunks pulled out by idle, bored, spiteful hands.

Max threw on their high-vis vest and strapped the velcro together. They checked the computer to see the schedule for today. In about ten minutes, there'd be the first ship. It was marked "Maritime Dynamo." Max sighed, staring at the screen.

"More automatons for the Spire," they said. It was matter of fact, defeated. More people would be replaced, be sent scampering for whatever dirt they could scratch a living out of.

"Aren't those the guys who make those real human-lookin' ones? You know, the ones people use as maids and shit?" Joseph stared down at the screen.

Max nodded. "Yep. They're the ones the Spire jerks love so much." Speaking a bit more freely than before, knowing there were at least a few inches of concrete between them and any camera's microphone.

Joseph stroked his chin fuzz. "It's always felt a little mocking. 'Look at us, fuckin' richer than god, we don't even need people anymore,' and all that. Seriously, this shit," he tapped the screen, "it was a fucking omen. We should have done like the luddites and cracked them to pieces."

"I don't know if that would help," Max said. "It's just so damn tiring. They want us to work and work and work. Keep talking about how we're building a future and, y'know, we might be, but none of this feels like it matters. None of it's worthwhile. I just want something that matters."

"Ah, yeah," Joseph said. "I'm sure that'll happen real soon." Max felt the snide mockery slinking inside. They shook it off— Joseph being Joseph. The Federation was talking about better deals, about striking, about fighting for better wages and better conditions. That was enough, at least for Max.

"Joe, can we talk about this later?" Max asked. With the ever-present risk of someone overhearing, it wasn't wise to keep talking.

He smirked and nodded. "Of course. We have work to do after all. Maybe this day'll be a bit different from *all* the shitty days before, huh?"

"Asshole," Max laughed.

Max and Joseph were met outside by Franklin, their boss. Wearing a long-sleeved button-up shirt that did almost nothing to hide his military cyberware, he looked like a mix of veteran, corporate stooge and regular family man. He was a middle manager, took care of a few of the sectors but largely just walked around to show everyone the bosses were watching and was not himself ... the best boss, in Max's estimation. Perhaps not evil or conniving but too much of a corporate hound to do anything besides bark upper management's orders. And it was always annoying to have to shut up and be somewhere-adjacent-to-respectful around him, but such was life.

"Hey, boss," said Max, giving a wave as they got within earshot. Franklin waved back with a silver hand.

"Morning," he said. "This coming shipment's looking to be pretty important for the next phase of the Automated Future

Plan. I'm sure you're all up to the task. Have you been looking at the exciting opportunities?"

Max couldn't tell if that was sarcasm or corporate-required speak. It might have been both—Franklin and they had never spoken outside of work, and the conversations were confined to the mundane topic of shipments and crates. But the tone: Max couldn't place it. They had the expected, corporate-approved answer ready.

"Yeah," they said. Lying through their teeth, they continued, "Yeah, I've been looking at the stuff on Io—apparently they're looking for skilled technicians and I figured I could at least apply. I don't know if I meet the education requirements, but I don't see the harm in trying."

Franklin nodded sagely. "Of course, no harm in trying. You dropped out, right? They can look past that sometimes if you can show you have the skills they need."

'Max cringed a little. They had dropped out in their second year. Computer science. Learning how to code and program. They had told Franklin that—god, it must have been months ago and only the once. He'd remembered, of course. Of course, he'd remembered.

"Yeah, but I still had a few projects under my belt by then. I worked internships with a few companies, and I still have the contact information if I need people to vouch for me."

"Good luck, Max," he said. This, Max knew, was genuine. Warm. He knew, well as anyone, what was coming. He knew that this was probably one of the last times he'd be talking to Max. "We're all building futures together, and that includes our own."

So much talk of future. So much talk of building something better. It all rung hollow to Max. The whine of klaxons filled the air, and a loud, automated voice declared booming, "Dock Three: incoming vessel. Docking procedures initiated."

The huge gate opened, and Max stepped back. It was an instinctive response, born out of fear. The one day that shit hadn't worked, that the docking procedures had failed and things broke down was now branded into their brain. More muscle memory and emotion than recollection, they remembered that day in small doses. Grinding, snapping steel, sparks flying and the threat of decompression. Crying in the breakroom because they had been told they couldn't leave—shifts never ended early. The whole dock had been shut down for a few hours as the situation was resolved. The traffic that had built up was hell. The docking of their pay hurt. But they were thankful they didn't lose their job.

Even after that incident, the repairs the company had made were minor. Nothing more than what was needed to keep the traffic flowing. There was never time, never the resources needed to shut down the whole section. Commerce moved too fast, too blindingly fast, for there to ever be a chunk of time to allot to the days of repair.

But the gate opened now without incident. The seals worked and the back of the shuttle split apart. There were a few dozen shipping containers. Max and Joseph got to work in the ordained fashion—top to bottom, left to right. Instead of clambering over the containers, up ladders and such, they did it the right way. Bringing out that old scissor lift, Max drove over and raised themselves up, attaching the guide points. Magnetic hooks slowly slid the container off its companion. The sound of lightly greased metal sliding off itself grated against Max's ears. Along the ceiling, magnetic hooks descended and attached themselves in conveyor-like fashion, sending the crate along the path to its destination. To be unpacked, its contents spilled out into the infinite shipping lines that crisscrossed the station, either in dedicated transport vehicles or by more basic tubes and conveyors.

Max often wondered just how arterial the station was, how connected it all could be. Obviously, quite a bit—the automation already present was mostly for transport and shipping around the station, bringing goods to and from the Spire and around the different sectors. But how many tunnels, nooks, crannies existed that they would never see?

Franklin watched with impatient nosiness. Max heard him talk to Joseph, telling him to hurry this up or quicken that up. Thirty minutes for a full unloading, and they were at ten already. It wasn't Joseph's fault—he was hardly taking his time. Max could see him at work on the magnetic hooks, ensuring they were safe, making sure they worked, that the power was connected to each one. He was following procedure and still being chastised for being too slow.

Franklin didn't seem to pay that much attention to Max, but why? Maybe he was being nicer to them, without meaning to. Or maybe they just weren't within proper viewing distance, their errors left unseen and unmentioned. Who knew?

Thirty-two minutes and the unloading was done. The next ship was due in three minutes. How the hell could they expect, with any fucking reasonable certainty, that half an hour was enough turnaround time for this sort of work?

Fourteen more ships and nine more hours of work before their shift ended. One more increment and they would qualify as full-time workers, after all. And so finally, they left, bidding Franklin farewell. He had stopped watching them long ago, instead answering emails on a laptop and sitting idly off in a corner, taking up one of their chairs so that one of them was always left standing on the few breaks they had. Sitting on the floor was, after all, breaking some sort of regulation hidden away deep in the rulebooks.

"Come on, let's go to the bar," Joseph said. "I need a fucking drink."

"Do you?" They had seen how much Joseph drank. It was ... concerning. Charming when they were in university together and Max tried to outdrink him, but they had been the buzzed friend helping their plastered friend back to his apartment far, far too many times.

"*You* do," Joseph said. "Lighten up a bit! We're probably not going to get many more chances, after all." That cynical statement put a thought in Max's head. They ... maybe they could check with Franklin. Ask for a bit of help or assistance if it all went wrong.

"Okay," Max sighed. "Can you give me a minute? I'll meet you at the bar."

"What, Max? You don't wanna leave Vic waiting."

"I'll be a few minutes," they said. "Promise, I'll be there before you're done with your first drink."

"Bold promise."

Max sighed deeply and steeled themselves. They started toward Franklin, rolling ideas in their head. How to ask, how to express themselves. Do they go in confidently, handshake and all, and say they needed to discuss something? Or casual, like a friend? Or a family member?

It would be fake no matter what. If they wanted to be honest, it would be tears and ugly sobs and demands. It would be anger and spite. It would be resignation to his power over them, hoping that he didn't fire them on the spot for ... pleading for help was the right way to put it, really. They remembered the little pods that the people without jobs were afforded, the dehumanizing mercy they were granted. Pens with a mattress, stacked one after the other, rented out and added to your debts, if you couldn't pay. It was billed as a mercy, but they always told people they could do better if they didn't rely on handouts. But here, Max had to at least ask for help. A referral, a contact, a piece of advice.

"Hey, Franklin," they said as they approached. He looked up from his laptop, scratching his stubble-covered face.

"Yeah, Max?"

"So, about the, uh, opportunities." They put their hands behind their back to hide the shaking. They struggled to get the words out. Were they being some sort of traitor? Not trusting in Joseph, the Federation, the planned strike? Or was this just a contingency, in case of the worst? It didn't mix well with them, not at all, to be talking to Franklin and planning to meet Victoria minutes later. But still, they pressed on. "I was just wondering if, uh—I've been working here for about two and a half years. Is there anything you can point me to? People you think I should contact, referrals I can get?"

"Max ..." he sighed and folded his laptop up. "You're a good kid, but that's kind of in breach of company policy, isn't it? We're meritocratic here, after all."

"Sir, I don't want to puff myself up, but we've worked together for years. If there's a meritocracy, you've seen my merits, right?"

He nodded. "Yeah, I have. You're good at unpacking stuff. You're good at loading crates. You're good at emptying ships. I've seen what you're good at, and you're talking about applying for jobs that I've never seen you do. What do you want me to do? Put your name out for others to peruse? There's going to be a thousand people like you, and they'll all have merits, too."

A particularly bitter bile built up in the back of Max's throat. They wanted to scream something, to ask if their years of diligence and work had meant nothing if they couldn't even ask for a favor or ask him just to help out or ... anything! Here Max was, dancing on the precipice, about to lose a job, about to be sent off somewhere deeper, more thankless, more hopeless, and the best that could be offered was this?

"Take the new opportunity as a chance to, well, show others your new merits, reinvent yourself a little. If I moved some pieces, pulled strings to you get a job, then you'd stagnate."

"But, sir," they stopped themselves before it became groveling. "I understand. Sorry to bother you. Can I still call you up if someone needs a reference?"

"Of course, Max. I'll vouch to your company spirit any day of the week. But that's all."

Chapter Two

The Screwdriver was a fun little place. Half impromptu union hall, half bar and only about three-quarters in compliance with station regulations, it was shunted off to the furthest corner possible of the sector, facing outward to the starfield and sun. It was between a storage area and a viewing gallery that would let people lounge and watch the stars ... for whatever reason. Probably just to give the illusion of recreational space. The thick windows would darken when facing the sun, preventing the worst of the solar radiation, but it still wasn't particularly pleasant.

It felt a little alien when the lounge faced the starfield. So many tiny pinpoints of light, in such different arrangements than on Earth. No constellation looked familiar; nothing except the orbiting bodies of the solar system looked even remotely familiar. And even those were too far away to really register. Not that it stopped Max from trying to create a new constellation every time they passed. Most of them ended up cosigned to the noble names of "Blobbus Maximus" and "Blobbus Minimus."

Tonight's bouncer outside the Screwdriver gave them a stern look, peering with artificial eyes. She was a familiar sight, with fiery red hair that was *absolutely* dyed and augments that made her day job of spacewalking and examining the station's countless seals easier, artificial eyes to scan in minutia, arms of plastic and steel that could hold on to a handrail floating in space for hours without tiring. Max, for a moment, became aware of all their own tiny augmentations and changes.

A pay-pad on their palm, connected to their LMC bank account. A small neurological aid that helped them regulate their circadian rhythm in the station. Another that helped with balance in case spacesickness took over or the station shifted in an unusual way—a matter of when and not if, Max discovered. They shook off the thought and just fist-bumped the bouncer when she approved Max's entry into the bar.

Across the bare concrete floor, the angular, blunt plastic benches and chairs and the tables made of faux granite and linoleum, lights sparkled. Moving disco balls, each with glowing lightbulbs, rotating, twisting, mixing red and green and blue and yellow and a dozen more colors, hung from the ceiling. Max had heard, in the drunken sort of rumormongering that goes on, that they had been installed to hide how bad the food actually looked under proper white light. Having, unfortunately, tasted it on one of the chef's off days, they could believe it.

Passing by a neo-Brutalist fixture that jutted in such a way that it seemed designed out of malice toward the drunken, Max ran into a meter-high, off-white cylinder. It moved smoothly through the bar, a small stalk on top carrying its single eye. Stopping in front of Max, its single eye bore down on them. A dented bronze nameplate shone with kaleidoscopic light: Gerry Rigg, Bartender.

Its tinny voice sounded out, synthesized in the moment through entirely outdated programs and software. "Identity:

Max Caldwell. Please choose a location. Service shall be rendered shortly."

"Hey, Gerry," Max said. "I'm just gonna sit over here," they gestured over to a table in the corner. Joseph was there, sitting and brooding over a beer. "If that's okay."

The robot's answers were preprogrammed, but there was still this compulsion to reply. It was nice to do, and Max had noticed over the years that a pretty good tell of someone's personality was how they treated the robot. Assholes tended to knock it around; most people just ignored it as a fixture or replied simply to it, as if thinking aloud, using Gerry as a sounding board.

"Max! You finally fuckin' made it, huh?" Joseph lit up, straightened himself out. "Don't know what's taking Vicky so long. Sure hope she's alright, but I wouldn't worry about it."

"She's not here?" Max furrowed their brow and sat down. "Damn. Yeah, hope she's okay." They shifted their backpack to the side, the various wires and electronics settling down into a tangled mass. "I just hope she trusts me."

"I'm vouching for you, don't worry," Joseph said. "This isn't exactly something we do all the time, but there's guidelines and shit for a reason. There's not a lot of blackhats on the station. Vicky's interested in talking to you for that reason."

Blackhats—that was, they supposed, the closest thing to a title they had. A hacker who specialized in infiltrating security systems, in person or remotely. Max preferred the in-person method, with wires and laptops and the ability to access hardware physically. It wasn't easy or fun or particularly profitable work—they had never been able to crack into something like corporate RnD documents. At least not yet. But it had its uses, particularly when certain niches opened up, as when people needed tune-ups and the cyberware companies started charging more and more for what, by all accounts, should have been free updates and maintenance. How it wasn't criminal was beyond Max, but each exemption and skirt around the law paid for itself, at the end of the day.

Max didn't hear the person walk up behind them and pat them on the shoulder. The grip was firm, solid. A woman with short curling hair sat down across from Max. In the shifting light, Max tried their best to take stock of the woman; a white t-shirt, one sleeve torn off to reveal a black-and-white mechanical left arm that ended just under the shoulder, with its abrupt transition from mechanics to brown skin. The lights reflected off the plastic, off casing and soft synthetic tissues. It was hard to tell what model the arm was in the dim light. The woman spoke.

"Hello." Max could hear the exhaustion of work in her voice. It was all too familiar, even in this stranger. "I'm Victoria."

"Wondering where you were," Joseph grinned, taking a long sip from his beer. "What held you up?"

"Nothing special. Now, this is ...?"

"Oh, uh, I'm Max. Joseph said he told you about me, I'm —" nervousness shot through Max's body. They, unthinkingly, extended a hand to shake. Again, Victoria's grip was firm. Her eyes narrowed. Had they already fucked this up?

"They're the local blackhat and cybersurgeon," Joseph interjected. Max retracted their arm. Of course, they would be the type to stumble this early on.

"Surgeon might be a little far, I mean—"

Joseph cut them off again, stopping them right at the start of their self-deprecation. Maybe it would play well to Victoria, maybe they could get on her good side.

"Like fuck you aren't!" Joseph laughed. "You look at body parts that don't work right and make 'em work again. That's surgery, isn't it?"

Victoria shook her head. "This arm's slowed down a little. Nothing major, but I can tell. It's already made my week hell. I know the company released a new patch or model or something in the software for it, only it'll cost me about seventy-five bucks to get it. Can you save me those seventy-five?"

For a moment, Max thought about what they were doing here. They wanted to help Victoria, but a knot in their stomach told them this was a step too far. If they didn't make a good impression, then what? Would they just need to consign themselves to doing nothing? They knew damn well they were a good hacker, that they could put pressure on the right points, could worm through security and understood how computers worked on a fundamental level. And they knew they could help make life a bit more bearable. But it came down to Victoria liking them. That was their one in with the militants. If they failed, the alternatives were few and none of them seemed good.

"Do you know your model?" Max asked. "Aegis, Daedalus, what is it?" As they got their laptop out and started untangling the wires, their mind shifted. The nervousness melted away a bit, though it still hung around them, slinking in the shadows of the mind. It was time to work—they could, at least, help out a bit here. Even if Victoria decided that they weren't ... enough for the PF, then at the very least they could help her here.

"Yeah, it's a Daedalus ... uh, XM-97."

"Old," Max commented. "Tough, though. If it wasn't for these damned updates and stuff, you could keep it most of your life. Probably pour acid on it and it'd be fine."

Victoria smirked. "Trust me, I have."

"Ah ..." Max didn't want to push further. "Do you want to take it off? I know some people don't like me reading biometrics. It's nothing revealing, just neural connections and basic stuff like that."

"Of all the days to do it, I forgot my hex keys," she joked. "I don't suppose you have any?"

"Okay, just asking," Max put up their hands. "I might have them, if you actually want to." They waited a moment. Victoria made no motion, just kept looking them up and down. She was trying to get a feel for them, and Max looked to see if there was any indication, any sort of inkling they could glean. In the confusing light, nothing. Max started looking through their files, the latest ones obtained in a data leak from Daedalus Industries and all of their different sister companies. They came constantly: leaks from within, from without, the constant arms race between code-crackers and security programmers. Every few weeks, Max woke up with a new link in one of their secured communications, to packages of encrypted files sometimes tens of gigabytes big. When you really looked, though, a lot of it was bloat for fundamentally small updates and patches and such. Maybe a hundredth of what was in each update was useful. Nonetheless, they always paid for them on time, transferred it into their accounts, but nearly each expense turned into profit before the next update.

"So," they thumbed over a file with a name mostly comprised of numbers: XM-97.11.12—the latest update. "I think I have it." They handed a cord over to Victoria.

"So," Victoria plugged it into her arm, "I suppose we shouldn't beat around the bush any longer. Joseph said you wanted to meet me. Why?"

"Oh, uh." Max froze, staring at the screen of their laptop.

"Joseph didn't tell you about my time with the Jericho Collective? I worked with them on their penny-slicing operations. I set up the attack that let them slip into the local cryptobank." The memory brought with it a twist in the gut. They'd been rooming with four other people, huddled into a small room that was almost always too hot, too stuffy to be comfortable. They still had the taste of cheap chicken ramen in their mouth all these years later. Somehow, they were still happier then than now. Maybe that was the rose tinting of time and nostalgia. They looked up at Victoria, who was watching Max intently. They took that as a sign to continue. "They offered me a cut—nothing much, we only sliced off some few hundred satoshi in a week. I got a small share of that, but it kept me fed for a few months. I'm sure if you asked any of the Canadian members about a 'FallenMilton,' they'd remember."

"FallenMilton?" Victoria asked.

"I was really into poetry back then," Max sheepishly admitted. They looked down at the screen. "Transfer's done. File's ready. If you're ready, I'll just reboot your arm and you should be good to go."

"What do I owe you?" Victoria asked.

"Nothing," Max said. It was a lie—normally they'd ask for ten, fifteen bucks. Do a few of these a month and be able to pay for the latest package's encryption keys and keep this business going. But *pro bono* was hardly unheard of.

"Kind of you," Victoria smiled. "I assume we're done here?"

Max thought for a moment. "Yeah," they said. "I think we're done here. It was nice meeting with you, Victoria. I hope we meet again soon."

"I'll be in touch."

Chapter Three

Every day felt empty. With a grunt and a moan, they pulled themselves out of bed. Plodded to work, ate when they could. Each stare from the guards made a shiver of paranoia crawl down their spine. Each day ended with disquieting silence. Joseph and them spoke almost every day. About small things, frustrations or idle chatter about whatever was in the crates. Almost every day, Max would nearly venture asking about Victoria. They pulled back each time, changed the topic.

More parts for more machines came in. More computers, more drones, more things entirely named in alphanumeric with a company name listed beside it. One shuttle rolled into port and contained nothing but steel shipping containers marked in the computer system as "LEGS." In a flicker of levity, Max and Joseph joked about stiletto-wearing, fishnet-bound automatons. That spark faded and work returned in its stead.

From time to time, Max thought their phone buzzed with a message from a friend or thought their computer had pinged them with a message from family, sent across the millions of miles. The former was just an update on phone bills, the latter advertisements sent to them by the company. Once their buzzing phone surprised them. Instinctively, hoping to be wrong, they checked the message. Spiderweb cracking over the phone screen obscured words, but they only needed to see that it was a nameless number to know it was worth ignoring. They shoved their phone back into their pocket and carried on.

They kept thinking about Victoria. They played their own words over and over in their head, hoping that they came across as anything but uncertain. They kept thinking about her words, also—illegal shit sometimes, fights sometimes. Could they stand up to *anyone* in a fight? Were they diving too deep into something? These anxieties rotted in their guts. The only thing that kept them from utter boredom was tense nervousness.

One day, they finally laid down on the bed, letting out a deep sigh as their weight settled on the mattress. With some relief, they tried to think of what to do tomorrow. No shift was scheduled, but in some ways, that was just a little more painful. Nothing to do, no structure. Most everyone else would be working. Joseph was. The day would be structureless, undefined. Everything they did would need to be kept within company-set or financial bounds, and neither left a lot to do. The relief left them and they lay in bed, waiting for sleep.

There was a knock on the door. Max shuffled out of bed. An apocalyptic voice inside them whispered, telling them this was a mistake. Security had caught up to them, someone had tipped someone off—who knew what was behind the door? They adjusted their sports bra in the darkness. It took every ounce of muscle to get up, to break from the hold the bed had on them. Step by step to the door, they grumbled something and opened it.

"Oh," Joseph looked away. "Shit, didn't mean to wake you."

"Joe ...?" They yawned a little and rubbed their eyes. When

their sight focused, they saw Joseph was covered head to toe. Thick black jacket and sweatpants, boots, a balaclava pulled up over his head, he looked like a moving shadow. In his nylon-gloved hands, he was concealing something. "What're you doing here? Isn't it like ... five in the fucking morning?"

"Last minute preparations. Don't worry about it. Actually, no: do worry about it. It's important. Can I come in?"

Light seared Max's eyes as Joseph stepped in and flicked the switch. The door behind him closed. Max heard the sound of weight settling onto their squeaky couch and when they finally opened their eyes, on their squat little coffee table were three zip-lock bags, each half filled and labeled messily. Little cotton balls were stuffed into the two bottom corners of each bag.

"It's not, you know, professional and all that. That one's called 'spiro' or something, that one's ... 'estra'-something," Joseph mumbled his way through the barely remembered pharmacology. With a burst of energy, Max seized the orange bottle beside their bed, the few pills shaking in their rush to read the label. The bottle read "estradiol 30 × 20mg."

"Where the fuck did you get these?" Max breathed out. *Breath in—deep, slow. Get your bearings. Don't collapse.* It looked like in that one bag alone, two, maybe three months' of Max's HRT. The label on the ziplock read "estradiol ≈400 × 20mg." "Where the *fuck* did you ...?"

His laugh was halfhearted, barely audible. "Victoria works chemical. Knows people in pharmaceutical. A few dozen medications we figured we'll need went conveniently missing. Don't need to ask too many questions about it. But I guess Victoria felt you deserved a bit more than recognition. Tit for tat, I suppose."

"Joe, I ..." they sat down, hand shaking. With as much care

as they could muster, they cracked open their plastic bottle and counted the pills. Three and a half chalky, white-blue pills left, 20mg each (save for that broken one). "This is months, fucking *months* of ..."

They trailed off and put the bag down on their bed. They breathed in and out slowly. Trying to find words.

"What do I owe you?"

"Jesus, Max. Nothing. Didn't you hear me say that this was pay for what you did?" He sighed. "Did you get Vic's message?"

"Huh?"

"She sent you a text earlier," he crossed his legs and leaned back. "Wondering if you got it. It'll be cryptic, might not look like much. Maybe spam detection caught it?"

Max picked up their sweatpants, lazily thrown on the ground before they went to bed and rifled through them. They ran their finger across the cracked screen, opening up the text messages. From an unknown number, there was a single text. It was long, winding, and something Max would have absolutely ignored. Had absolutely ignored.

The gist of it was asking if they'd decided to attend a party for someone's retirement. Confused for a moment, they read deeper, thought a little longer. The date was tomorrow, the time impossibly early. *Celebrate the retirement of a manager* ... it clicked.

"Strike's starting tomorrow," they whispered. "No," they corrected themselves, "Today. Two hours from now. Shit, I ... I missed it. I'm sorry. I'm so sorry, I—"

"You coming or not?"

They put down their phone carefully. Silence hung heavy for a moment as a thousand thoughts raced through their mind. As their heart drummed furiously, words spilled from their mouth.

"I planned on being there, Joseph, I promise I was planning on being there. I didn't see the message until now. You didn't need to make sure I was gonna go. I wasn't going to flake or—"

"Are you trying to convince me or yourself?"

The questioned stopped them dead in their tracks. Waves of disgust, worry and embarrassment washed over them. "Myself," they admitted. "I'm sorry."

"I have to go now, Max. There's a lot of work to be done. Get some more rest. Seven a.m. *today*, got it? We have a job for you now."

Sleep was impossible after that. They lay in bed staring up at the ceiling and just waited. Their heart wouldn't calm down, their legs and arms kept twitching. Tighter and tighter, they wound themselves up with apocalyptic thoughts. Every way it could go wrong. They half expected to hear a second knock on the door, to be taken away somewhere to be interrogated.

Max got up and made themselves a cup of coffee. Their little single-serve coffee maker was complimentary when they got their apartment. The pods were not complimentary and, even if one factored in the saved travel time, horrendously overpriced. As they brushed their fingers over the labels and selected a French Vanilla pod, they knew this wouldn't help their nerves at all. But the coffee was brewing: they were acting more on impulse. It felt strangely right to get ready for today the same way they would any other, if only because familiarity kept them from spiraling.

They put on their usual outfit, throwing on a black sweater, white tank top and off-gray sweatpants that they hoped looked clean, drank their coffee quickly and rooted through their mini-fridge for food. A prepackaged salad, slightly wilted, would have to do.

When they got to the docks, it was busier than they ever could have expected. Barely past six and it was bristling with people. Some they recognized, most they didn't. On some level, this made sense to Max. People always loved signing up to do shit when the chance came. Strike committees, distribution groups, propaganda spreaders.

Why was it called propaganda? *Agitprop* or something, if they were being weird about it. It was a terrible name. Might as well name yourself the Totally-Not-Evil People. Of course, if you asked anyone, they'd say they were *countering* propaganda. But still.

It wasn't long until yet more arrived. Dockworkers with their lists of grievances. Soon, the dock was full of people. Some put banners up. A striking, plain flag—red and black made of shining polyester—was hung over the rail that normally guided boxes away on maghooks. A few people brought signs, hastily made or old and broken out of storage for the event. Others still carried in boxes full of water, granola, coffee, whatever food they could bring to the table. Max picked a chocolate bar when offered.

And so it began. Twitching and pacing between groups of people, flitting from place to place, incapable of stillness. A few times, they overheard people hyping themselves up, reminding themselves and others that it'd go well, that the company was probably reasonable, that there were more of "us" than "them." But that wasn't much comfort: the various companies had shattered strikes before. After a few sloppy attempts, most companies had become well versed in the subtle art. They themselves had seen it in person, back when they were still planted on solid ground and breathing unrecycled air, when the stakes involved were an abstract concept. There was a drive at the local coffee shop just outside their university. An attempt to unionize, to strike for better wages. It was a small franchise and they had been going there for months every morning, knew a bunch of the employees on a first-name basis. Those employees got fed up. Angry. Max, for their part, had donated to the fund. But it didn't work in the end.

It took only a week for their replacements to get Max's order right without asking.

Someone gripped them by the shoulder. It felt like ice spreading through their body. Air forced its way down their throat, a half gulp that spread an awful pain through their chest.

"Yo, Max. Glad you made it. Got a second?" Joseph asked. Their heart was still racing, their body still clenched, but at least they were able to reply.

"What's up?"

"Told you we had things for you to do. How do you feel about getting your hands a bit dirty? Me and some other PFs were having some pretty chill conversations," and by his expression alone they knew that meant he had probably been shouting at someone. His voice, come to think of it, had a bit of a harsh edge to it. Strained, grated. "And we figured it'd be a right lot of fun to fuck up the automatons they wanna replace us with. Nothing permanent, promise. Only problem is, not many of us know computers. Until I pointed out that I know just the lil' hacker who could help us out."

Max furrowed their brow. "So ... you're asking me?"

"If you feel down for some pro bono mild vandalism of company property."

"I'm not ..." Max stuttered out. For a moment, their impulse was to say no. But then why did they meet Victoria? They let it rumble around in their head for a moment and realized it must have gone well. This was them getting the chance they wanted. "Why? Can't just be for kicks."

"No, it's because they're still operational, big as fuck and full of drones. They could be activated during the strike and how'd that look?" He grinned. "It's not like we need any more problems right now. But, hey, I won't bend your arm over it if you're a lil' scared. I get that." That grin, that acidic underlying sarcasm. It needled in, that tense, disgusting feeling of needing to show someone up. Was he ... trying to provoke that? Did he even know?

"Fine," they said. The corrosion had eaten through whatever barriers they'd had. Besides, it would make things easier for the strikers, make everything go more smoothly. And, they figured, that was reason enough to help.

"Great! I think Vicky's already poking around there."

The automatons were kept off in a corner, out of their crates and mostly assembled. They were huge structures, each the size of a shipping container and supported on eight legs, with pristine white plastic covering matte black hydraulics. It was arachnoid in appearance, with two legs supporting a front compartment big enough for only a few people, a thorax that housed all the guts that made it functional, and a massive abdomen that held all manner of things. Cranes bristled up from each of the abdomen's corners and Max could see the outlines of drone ports flush with the casing of the automaton. It was all in that neo-post-hyper-modern-whatever-the-fuck style that dictated the only two colors that existed were white and black, the only shapes were triangles and hexagons arranged into a tessellating array of mechanisms and machine learning. There were names written on the front of each automaton, under the pilot's chair—they were autonomous, yes, but a pilot could still take control if they wanted.

The first one was named Vulkan. Max could see the vinyl nametag peeling.

Victoria was leaning against the Vulkan, playing with some sort of fidget toy. She was wearing a hoodie and jeans, covering as much of herself as she could. If she had to run, Max figured, at least her most obvious features would be concealed. Against the massive machine, she looked tiny—all six-and-a-bit feet of her were overshadowed by the single leg-joint she was against.

When the two were close enough for her to see their faces, she remarked, "Joseph, you got them? Good. Did he tell you what's up?"

"He said something about wanting to fuck up the machines?" Max offered. Victoria smirked, pocketed the little toy and stood upright. She moved without nervousness, without fear. This was routine. Or it was being treated as routine.

Victoria made a "so-so" gesture. "More or less. We figured now would be a good time to make sure we actually cut their hands off. If the dock here is shut down and the automatons are down, it becomes a game of chicken."

"Chicken?"

"Either we give up or Ashe gives in. This station has six months of supplies. No one here has a private spaceship with which to run except for maybe the top two or three jackasses. So sure, Ashe might get cold feet and go home, but then he'll have shareholders, wealthy investors, and probably a bunch of retirees who wanted to die peacefully looking out at the stars all saying he's abandoned them. I think that'll at least nudge things in our direction." She explained this all calmly, coolly. Max nodded along as though they were completely cool with all of this. As though they didn't have their hands deep in their pockets, hoping Victoria couldn't see them trembling.

"Won't that hurt the negotiations? The company will see us as being unreasonable." Max asked. Victoria shrugged.

"Look, we can't trust them to be reasonable. I am not asking you to blow something up. I'm asking you if you can help us out by taking a few cards out of the company's deck."

They thought for a moment.

"Okay," Max said. "What precisely do you want me to do? I've not really worked with automatons before, but they're computers with robot bits and I know how both computers and robots work." They didn't think they were lying, but there was still that little voice whispering all the ways this could go wrong.

Victoria shrugged. "How do we disable them long enough to make sure the company can't set them up but without tearing out wires? That's your job, I guess."

Max thought for a moment. That was a fairly precise order—there's not many ways to make a functional computer refuse to work, not unless you break some pretty specific things.

"I guess the terminal is in the pilot's seat? If we look up there, we might be able to find its router, connections and stuff. Remove those and the thing's cut off from remote control." As they explained, Max's anxiety morphed, shifted a little. It became a lightness in their chest, pushing them up, the words out. They were *actually* doing this. "O-oh, and if you wanted to make it so that you couldn't use them flat out, you could try interrupting a factory reset. That might be possible. It wouldn't brick them, but it'll buy time even if they manage to get someone in the cockpit to start it up. Hours to reinstall, at least."

The answer made Victoria smile. She looked up and down at the automaton. "I can help you, if you want. It'll be easy, all these things are identical anyways," she said.

"I'll need to see the OS first. I might need your help with the other stuff too. I don't want to take up too much of your time, though, so if the first one goes easy, maybe I can do the rest myself?"

"Maybe," Victoria didn't sound too convinced. Max realized, perhaps a little late, that this was a test. To see if they could be trusted.

Max took a moment to admire the automaton, this giant beast of steel and plastic, code and flickering digital intelligence. Art had never much taken Max's attention, but these were as beautiful as any statue they had seen, and the thought of them in motion was threatening and awe-inspiring in equal measure.

Up they climbed. Carefully, slowly, up the stairs, until they got to the cockpit. Two chairs, one for pilot and the other for copilot. It was cramped, a little uncomfortable. The back of the chair seemed designed not for lounging but to keep you upright. Stable, focused. Uncomfortable enough that work was a welcome distraction.

No amount of white pleather would fix how much it sucked to lean back and try to relax in those chairs.

They pressed the big red start button. The whole machine rose to life. Batteries deep within its core hummed with the characteristic, animalistic purr of electrical machines. No combustion engines on this station. There was only so much air; burning was a waste.

Victoria entered the cockpit soon thereafter. She sat down beside Max and observed them working. It felt judgmental, Max had to admit, but they got to work. The screens in front of them, surrounded by uncountable gauges, buttons and switches, burst into pixelated life. The logos of Splitbrain Intelligence burst from the blackness, a grand display of color and lights that faded into a bisected whirlpool.

"SI-OS," Victoria noted dryly. "Do you know that one?"

"They produced a few machine-learning programs I've worked with. I know it well enough to know that ..." they pressed down the tilde key on the keyboard. Seconds passed.

"So," said Victoria, "you know what you're doing?"

"I know the rough outline of what I'm doing," Max admitted. "I know I can do this; it just might take a little trial and error. Sorry if Joseph oversold my abilities."

"He told me that you knew what you were doing. You seem to be proving it."

At a loss for words, they just concentrated on the OS. After tilde, the boot system would—yeah, there it was. A bright, almost painfully bright, blue with dark gray text. Whoever the fuck designed the UI deserved to be put against a wall and shot, honestly. It was painful to look at, to scroll through. Max patted to make sure their glasses case was tucked in the pocket under their breasts. They unzipped their hoodie, got their glasses, grabbed the sunglasses-lens attachment and put them all on.

Better. At least their eyes didn't want to evacuate their skull anymore.

The boot screen had the "Reinstall OS" option. One of those do-not-interrupt-this processes that was actually real damn easy to interrupt. And so Max did, setting the computer to restart. Once the progress bar displayed itself and ticked upward from 0.00 to 0.01, ever and slowly upward, they reached for the power button. The machine jittered and shook, hundreds of tons of steel and plastic responding to a single button press. And then it died.

It died gently. Batteries stopped whirring. Hydraulics relaxed.

A final electronic gasp as it all relaxed and the automaton locked into a deep, long sleep. Max let out a long breath they didn't know they'd been keeping in. The pilot's pod had gotten hot, humid. Was that true, though, or was it just them? Just their nerves around the job, probably. They unzipped their hoodie fully and took it off. A white t-shirt, damp with sweat, was underneath.

"Right," Max said. "Can you help me? This thing's got a super-computer in it, but it should have just one connection to the Internet. If you can keep the lid up for me, I'd appreciate it." They gently knocked the back of the cockpit. If their guess was right, it would open up into the computer. Enough space to crawl in, to do repairs—or damage, as the case may be.

Victoria held the lid up as Max wormed their way inside. Between the banks of computers, the humming fans, the strangely metallic smell of dust, they were looking for a part. It was just a little thing, close to a grate and easy to see with the antenna that emerged out of its chassis. They writhed and wormed inside, passing banks of computer parts that cost as much as one of their kidneys. That was always the comparison used by computer specialists with sly grins and a foreknowledge of how fascinating viscera were to the common student. *As much as a kidney*, the teacher points to a GPU. *As much as an eye*, gesturing toward a RAM stick. The black market pays well for the workings of a human and the guts of a computer both. Now they joked about selling their organs to LMC just to get the company's debt collectors off their back.

"Everything okay in there?" asked Victoria. Max noted a tenor of concern. They stretched, trying to look back and assure her, but all they could do in the tight space was shout out some vague affirmation that they hadn't gotten stuck.

They found the part and got to work unscrewing it. With the

help of a coin and an all-too-awkward angle for their elbow, they disconnected the router and pulled it down, laying it flatly against the floor and pulling the connector cord out.

Max wiggled out from the space and wiped the dust off them best they could.

"It's done?" Victoria asked. Max nodded. "Not too hard, was it?"

"Computers do what we tell them to do," Max said. "They're hard to understand but easy to wrangle once you do." They tried to keep up that facade of confidence, hoping Victoria wouldn't hear the nerves in their voice. "They're the perfect workers, really. Don't complain, get tired or anything like that. I guess that's why LMC prefers them to humans."

"These ones just joined our protest," Victoria patted the screen. "Let's hope they do their jobs."

"I wish my job was just sitting around and sleeping," Max said. "Wait it out until the negotiations are over, see how long it takes for the company to come to the table."

"You think they'll come to the table?" Victoria's question was sharp, direct, its tone harsh.

Max adjusted themselves in the seat, the discomfort of the anti-ergonomic chair flooding into their back.

"I mean, they have to, right? We're shutting down the docks. I remember the union chief talking about how that'll force negotiations."

Victoria sighed. "I'm glad you're that confident, Max."

"You don't trust the companies all that much?" They regretted how they phrased it. It wasn't like they trusted those corporations either, but at the very least using force against a few hundred people blocking up parts of a station would be bad PR, right?

"No," Victoria said. "I trust them far, far more than you do. I've seen their playbook before. I trust them to act by it again. It's all 'family' and 'peace' and 'cooperation' until we threaten their bottom line. Then it's 'We had no other choice,' and talk about anarchist actors and agitators and justifying all the bleeding people." Victoria's voice was low, tinged with anger. "For what it's worth, I'd love for it not to come to that. But I trust the companies to show their true faces. They want this place running; we're stopping it from running. If you don't want people with power to hurt you, there's precisely one maxim to follow: do not fuck with their money. And what, precisely," she knocked on the dead screen of the automaton, "do you think you're doing right now?"

Max looked down at their dust-covered hands and it started to creep in. That slow, rotting realization. This was get-sent-back-to-Earth-to-stand-trial serious. This was more than a job at risk. They waded in too fast, too hard, and now they were stuck in the mud.

They crept down the ladder and wandered over to the wall, leaning against it. Their face burned with a nervous heat. They let out a drawling "Fuck," and took a few minutes to compose themselves.

And then they got back to work. Walking away didn't seem like an option anymore, even if they felt sick to their stomach climbing up that ladder again. Neither spoke much as they worked on the others. There wasn't much Max could piece together for conversation.

The final automaton powered down, and Max let out a long sigh.

"I take it you don't feel great about this," Victoria noted.

"It's fucking scary."

"Always has been. But, Max," she leaned back in that chair, "at least it's over and you did good. I'm willing to vouch for you to the other PFs, if you still want in."

Max stayed quiet for a moment, letting the idea sink in. It wouldn't *just* be this sort of mission, and they already felt so, so small doing this. How long would it be until they felt confident enough to even give an answer?

"Can you give me a little bit to think about it?"

"You were the one who wanted to get in touch with me. Are you getting cold feet at the reality of it all?"

"Yeah," Max admitted.

"Makes sense," she grumbled. "I did, too, when I first started. I don't know how much time I can give you to answer, but you don't need to have your thoughts sorted right now. Let's talk later and get this over with now."

Max and Victoria descended the ladder one last time, standing back to dread and admire their work, respectively. Somewhere between the third and fourth automatons, they decided that the two jobs could be done at the same time—so long as the lid leading into the guts of the automaton got propped open with something. All in all, it took about a half hour to get all half dozen of them down.

Joseph was there, waiting for them at the bottom. His face burned with a giddy excitement, wide eyed and barely holding back a laugh.

"Jesus," he said. "That'll piss them off. Good job, you two." A firm slap against Max's back. They flinched. "Anything we need to add to the report when the meeting comes around or is 'We fucked their machines up,' good enough?"

"If Max wants in, I'm willing to be their second."

"'If'? Come on, don't tell me it's up in the air *now?* Of all times! No, it's a *'when,'* isn't it?" He scoffed. "But at least you two like each other. When's the next PF meeting?"

"Should be tomorrow or the day after. It depends on how well the defense goes," Victoria shrugged. "Personally, I voted for 'ASAP' but who knows what that means in reality."

"And how's the defense looking?"

"Not terrible, from what I heard."

The two of them broke off to discuss business, closing in together. Max stood off to the side, not sure if they were supposed to be party or not to what was being said. They followed along at a few arm's lengths, listening to two people discuss the details of a strike in euphemism and veiled statements. After a while, Joseph motioned to Max.

"Come on, let's go. They need bodies."

Chapter Four

A security officer with a megaphone was screaming. People were gathered in an unorganized throng, watching him and his two-dozen friends stand with shields and batons and ... fuck, it looked like super soakers? Max couldn't really tell from this distance. Victoria was watching with them, and Joseph had joined the strikers, trying to get them into a formation. There were a mix of shouts, orders, requests and commands from every side.

"Under the LMC contract, Section 7, Clause 23: Mass refusal to work will be considered an act of disobedience. Under Section 7, Clause 1, 'Disobedience': Attempts to unionize outside of the LMC Happy Family program is considered a breach of contract. Disperse. Return to work or face punitive action!" shouted the officer. No one paid him much heed, though.

Max stared out at the officers, all dressed in black, all equipped like they were ready to put down a full-fledged insurgency. There was something ... particularly disquieting to Max about these thirteen-or-so officers. They seemed ready to take on an army, not a bunch of people who just didn't wanna be fucked over. Each one looked like they were just salivating at the chance to fuck someone up. Just begging for an excuse.

"I hope PF-3 got to work," mumbled Victoria.

"What're they supposed to be doing?" Max asked.

"They're supposed to be cutting off the radio comms so these guys can't call for reinforcements. We can handle two, three dozen of ..." she gestured out to the wall of shields, "them. But if they called in the Spire? The people who have access to the real, proper guns and stuff? I don't like those odds. So, we snip off their ears, cauterize it while we get the chance. Now let's go down and see if we can help."

"Yeah," Max said. That familiar, oh so familiar, sense of fear and nervousness ate at them all over again. But they took a step with Victoria and then another. And then another. And over they went, down the stairs, to the crowd. They joined near the back. Victoria got to work, running around talking to people. Telling them what needed to be done. Max tried to listen and follow along. But it was a storm of chaos, hundreds of people shifting and moving and looking out at the cops, and no one really knew who would budge first. Victoria vanished into the crowd, and Max felt so, so, alone.

"You have one minute to disperse. This is a final warning!"

Fear seized Max. They didn't move an inch. Everything seemed to slow down, something that ... wasn't them, something that came from so deep inside, took over. There was the countdown, vocalized. Max tried to match them, figure out how long they actually had. The counting seemed fast. Intentionally so. *Fifty-five Mississippi, fifty-four Missi– fifty-three Mi– fifty-two...* Fuck.

Run. Run fast and far. Their body screamed at them to run, to abandon everyone. But they couldn't. It was like the crowd pulled them in, magnetic and inescapable. They didn't run. They moved into the crowd. Deeper and deeper as the countdown continued.

The message was repeated. Section this. Clause that. Contract signed. Bound by law, enforceable on the station by the UN Corporate Freedom Act of Twenty-whenever. *Ten. Nine.*

Max noticed some people around were wearing masks. Good, proper masks. The ones the engineers liked to use when working with the engines, the ones people couldn't access without a few connections, the work masks that could stop some chemical spilling out from the hardware that kept this whole damn station running from actually bothering you. And they started to feel very, very naked.

Those people in the masks congregated up near the front. They started shouting things back at the security guards. Max couldn't tell what, not in the cacophony of it all.

Where was Victoria? Fuck, where was she?

The world slowed down. Louder than any shout, any scream or noise or crowd, there was a single sound. It dominated everything, rose above the crowd. Commanded silence from everyone.

Clattering metal and a gaseous hiss.

And Max fucking ran. As yellow-green gas rose and curled up around people's legs, as the masked people moved forward, as chaos exploded. Their heart beat loud in their chest, blood pumped around their ears, drowning out everything but the sound of terror and panic. They ran, trying to weave their way through the crowd. They fell to the ground, catching themselves. Pain screamed through their wrist as they scrambled on the cold, concrete floor. Like an octopus out of water, limbs flailing wildly as they tried to get up, Max struggled. Someone grabbed them by the neck of their hoodie and pulled them upright. Their throat tightened. It felt like being strangled. Then they were shoved along the second they got on their own two feet.

Max never got a good look at who it was.

Someone beside Max was trying to get past, to get to the front. They were covered head to toe in black, wearing a mask and far more prepared than they were. Something bounced off the ground and smacked the person in the face. They crumpled like tissue on the ground, silent and prone. Fuck. Fuck, fuck! Were they dead? Max let them lay there. They weren't operating on logic, on compassion, on anything but the pure, primal fucking fear that coursed through their veins.

Covering their mouth didn't help. It snaked through their fingers, dug into their eyes. Away, they had to get *away*! Through haze and pain and fear, they kept looking for an escape. A few hundred meters away, another group of people amassed, flailing in the gas and trying to organize themselves. Max ran, shot off to the side and found something resembling safety in an alcove. They sobbed, snorted, sucked up snot and phlegm and bile as they cried their eyes out. Deep, involuntary breaths forced clean, burning air into their lungs. It fucking hurt, even if it was clean.

After what seemed like forever, someone interrupted Max's agony.

"Jesus fucking Christ, that's where you went!" Joseph shouted. His voice was muffled by the plastic and fibrous filters of his mask. It had a strange, underwater quality to it. "Fucking hell, you got hit right front and center, didn't ya? Can you speak?"

"Barely," Max coughed.

"Good enough. Smart on you getting out here—might have been trampled if you weren't careful. Fuck, we didn't expect the tear gas this early. Shame on us for thinking they'd follow escalation guidelines." He offered Max his hand. With damn near no effort, he pulled them upright. "Get up, do jumping jacks. Exercise helps clear your lungs or nose or something. They make the PMC trainees do it during chemical defense training."

Max didn't do jumping jacks, but they did wander, drunk with pain, until they started to feel a little more clear-headed, a little more sane. They took a long, deep breath, one that didn't hurt and then turned to Joseph.

"How'd you find me?"

"I didn't. You were in my way," he said. "Decided to check on you before I run off. I've lost a lot of time. Now, if you need a mask, I have a spare—I was passing them out before shit went down." He offered them a mask, grey and rigid plastic with a large faceplate. They put it on, adjusting the elastic around the back. It fogged up almost immediately. Joseph shook his head, annoyed. "Get the seal right. Stay safe." He left, running down the halls desperately.

Max looked out to the crowd and felt lost. For a moment they were stuck in indecision. They couldn't run into the crowd; they couldn't fight directly. They had never learned how to throw a punch, let alone go toe-to-toe with the cops. They couldn't sit back, watch it happen, be neutral. They took a nervous, tentative step. And then another. With each step they tried to make sense of their racing mind.

They needed to get a better look. They had to see what was going on. Up, up they ran to the second floor of the sector, to the catwalks that crisscrossed between the offices and the breakrooms and supply closets. A few others were up here, hanging out, clearing eyes and noses and observing. None of them paid Max much heed.

Looking down, Max saw the people shifting, moving. Security were being pressed, squeezed back into the hall. There was a constant shifting and moving of ranks, people slipping toward the back and being replaced by those moving forward. A wave, a constant rising, shifting wave. And only one side was advancing.

It wasn't long after that Max heard the general call to fall back. Everyone heard it. It practically echoed through the whole docks. What had been a solid block, a phalanx of moving men, collapsed into disorder as security broke and ran.

Max rushed down the stairs as people in the crowd dispersed, some to make sure the security didn't come back, others to take care of the hurt. Spent canisters and dropped shields littered the floor, the fans of the dock's ventilation systems moving and ridding it of the tear gas as people got to work. Joseph was there, handing out medical supplies, washing out eyes, trying to get people back on their feet. There was a twinge of guilt in Max for not having done more. They went over, asked how they could help. From there, they went around with a bottle of water in one hand and a bottle of painkillers in the other. A lot of people accepted them—dealing with split lips or bruises or black eyes.

It wasn't much, but it helped.

Soon after, the announcement came. Security had fled, been driven out of the sector. Sectors A, B, and D of the station were under union control. It was, at least for now, an occupation.

It really had gotten to that. After less than a day, the strike had gone from just sitting in their workplace and not working, to this. To a full-on occupation. That had always been, Max supposed, somewhere in the realm of possibility. They just never expected it, couldn't really *let* themselves expect it. They breathed out an uncertain sigh and went up to the main hall, following a small group up the stairs. A lot of them were as wide eyed, as shocked, as them. There were a few people with stony expressions, guiding others along. They seemed experienced or at least confident.

In the great main hall of the sector, there was a sense of disorganized order. No one was screaming orders at each other, but people were busy, working hard. Some started moving benches and tables, forming barricades at the obvious entrances. Others worked to shift chairs around, open wide spaces for people. Some were opening up the stores and restaurants, and people were settling down.

Max made their way over to a small café. Inside a few semi-familiar faces sat in the booths, directing whoever came in to just "Get whatever you want." For Max's part, that was a black coffee in a small paper cup.

They sat down on the edge of a fountain and decided to just ... let themselves enjoy this moment. The air felt electric, thin, exciting. As Max took gulps of bitter coffee, something tickled at their side. It was just a thought, poking, creeping in. Like an ivy at the window. They were excited.

Chapter Five

Max found Victoria sitting with a few other people near the center of the main hall, chatting about the day. With much relief, Max noticed that she seemed fine—not injured or anything quite too serious. As they approached, Victoria looked up and waved.

"Max, good to see you in one piece. I lost track of you, got a bit worried."

"I got tear gassed," Max said. "Joseph found me. I'm okay."

"Glad to hear you're okay," a slight smile crept on her face. "I'm just talking with some of the other PF leaders right now," she gestured to the people beside her. They were a mix of emotions, happy, dour, angry. All of them seemed just seconds away from a loud argument with each other. "Max here is a prospective member," she said, turning to her friends. "Helped disable the automatons with me and Joseph."

"Nice work," said one man, giving a curt nod. "Next meeting's today or tomorrow, whenever we lock this place down. Word'll be sent out. I'm James."

Max nodded cautiously. James knew what *prospective* meant, right? Max felt themselves freeze up a little at Victoria even telling these people about them. They said they wanted to join less than a few days ago. It was hardly official yet.

"Are you busy right now, Max?" Victoria asked. "Because I heard of something you might be able to help with, since this has just turned into something we measure in weeks. Apparently the computer systems in the agriculture section have become problematic."

"Oh," Max said. They felt like a ping-pong ball, bounced around and around but not stopping. It didn't really hurt too much, and they had to admit they were quite the opposite of busy—drinking coffee and sitting on various fountains. They would die for a little bit of rest right now. But instead, they said, "Agriculture? I know some folks up there. I can definitely check it out."

"Good," she said. "Having that place secure and working would be great. It means we'd be able to stretch our food supplies longer, maybe weeks longer. I'll see you later, Max."

There was a single elevator ride, albeit one at least a few minutes long, that Max had to suffer through to get to the agriculture section. Agriculture was in the tallest part of this sector, the top floors. Max had only been there for an interview when they first landed on the station—part of the required orientation and job placement—but that had been in a cold, white, sterile office.

The proper entrance to the agriculture section was through an airlocked chamber that came after the sterile neo-modernist, bare-bones office and lobby. A chemical sign labeled "Chlorophyll" marked the first set of white doors. Max stepped in front of them, and they opened slowly.

Entering the airlocked chamber, hearing the doors behind them close, Max wasn't entirely sure what to expect. The second set of doors to the agriculture section proper were an opaque black, and they opened gently, slowly, with a hiss.

It was beautiful. Max hadn't seen so much green in one place in years. Hundreds of hydroponic tubes running and crisscrossing back and forth, each stuffed to bursting with vibrant tomatoes or soybeans or some other bright vegetable. Swiss chard, in great, leafy bundles with striking red stems flopped out over the water, their roots flowing throughout the pipe network. Algae, intentionally and carefully cultivated within larger pipes and in thick, eye-level mats, smelled of earthy, still water and things Max thought had faded from their memory—of ponds and lakes at the park and still puddles after the rain.

They moved past tanks full of tilapia, lazily swimming in the water that fed them from excess algae and little flakes distributed by machine, their wastewater flowing into the pipes that fed the greens. Everything worked together in artificial harmony, stacked on top of each other in levels, bordered by catwalks and trails for inspection. From the fish at the bottom, to the algae above, and the leafy greens and vines on stainless steel trellises above that. Under the stairs and catwalks, planters lined their way around any bit of empty space. How could people manage all this?

Max got their answer when they saw a robot, a quadcopter drone, descend to one of the planters and fold up its wings. It moved along the dirt, stepping lightly on six snowshoe-like feet, plucking tiny clovers and weeds that had rooted themselves in the wrong place.

They sat down on the side wall of the array and watched the studious little robot work. It didn't care about the Federation of Unions or the fighting or security or anything. It had one job: to kill those weeds. And it did it efficiently, swiftly. A perfect worker.

Exactly what Ashe wanted. Exactly what the companies wanted. Max felt a little sorry for the robot—not that it had any feelings whatsoever. It had a purpose to fulfill, though. And that, it seemed, was enough.

Max's thoughts were interrupted by a small, open-topped and doorless cart rolling through the corridors. The cart held a single person, a short, red-haired woman whose face was almost instantly recognizable. *Sasha,* Max thought. Warmth spread through Max's body, a familiar comfort at seeing their old friend after so long. The cart came to a slow stop, and she stepped out. Wearing a pair of overalls and gloves, both stained and dirty, she smelled of compost and work.

"I'd hug you," she said with a smile, "but I just got finished mucking. Glad you got here. There's some stuff I'd like to talk to you about. Hope you didn't spend too, too long waiting?"

"No, no, I was just taking a look around. The little robots," they pointed over to the planters, "I guess I thought this place used something else."

"Oh, Hank's a good lil' guy," she gestured for Max to get into the cart.

"Hank?" Max stepped into the cart. The seats were cracked and worn, the paint chipped. This thing was very, very well used, but it glided over the concrete floor silently, smoothly.

"I name all the little weedbots. I have to load them up with batteries, make sure they're in proper working order, all that stuff. They're like my kids. Sort of. If kids were weed-killing robots."

"I heard there was something wrong and that I could help out. I assume it's something to do with computers or something?"

Sasha nodded. "Right. Something is borking up our robots. We've had to stop them from doing ... weird stuff like tearing up the plants. We're trying to open this place up so that the strikers can save non-perishables for later, keep everything going. Not like the station'll be receiving food shipments or anything. So, yeah, it's kind of bad."

"Alright. Show me them. Maybe I can see what's going on?"

The cart moved across the agriculture section swiftly, across repeating and repeating farm complexes. Lettuce, berries, growing cucumbers and squash hanging down in thick tendrils. It was an Eden on this station, as far as Max was concerned.

The cart came to a slow stop and Sasha got out to walk the rest of the way. Passing by one of the farming complexes on the final leg of the journey, Max may have discretely grabbed a few ripe strawberries off the plant when Sasha wasn't looking. They were sweet, tart, warm in the artificial grow light. The soft flesh practically melted away in Max's mouth. They hadn't had a strawberry, a good, fresh one that was neither in a squeeze tube nor needed water added to rehydrate, in a very, very long time.

The computer arrays that kept this whole place running seemed far more like Gehenna than Eden. It was dozens of server panels, all backlit a deep, pulsating red. The exhaust from the main computer was dumped somewhere else, not directly into the room, but the sheer radiant heat of a supercomputer running its trillions of calculations couldn't be entirely contained. The dehumidifiers, set up around the door, all roared with powerful fans. In this dry, hot, red hell, Max sat down in front of a computer screen and got to work.

The programs were unfamiliar, but they did a basic check. User interfaces all sort of coalesced around a few designs that worked so they were able to make some sense of it. An inbox, sets of orders, current statuses. And then came the order, marked

"Priority." A great flashing popup, dictating the orders that the company wanted done filled most of the screen. It took over a few seconds of scanning to pick out keywords: fallow the fields, drain the water, and overfertilize the earth was the gist of it all. They had thirty seconds until it auto-accepted. Max slammed the reject button as quickly as they could and let out a long, heavy sigh. It then asked for a reason. Max looked up at Sasha and motioned her over.

"Can you bullshit a reason?"

She nodded and took to typing up a long, formal address about how their boss, Lloyd, had gone out (or something, it was difficult to say as she had just showed up for work!) and she wanted to get *personal* authorization before carrying out such extreme and not to mention *profit-destroying* measures. Max threw in a few suggestions for good lines, veiled insults. The two of them worked hard to craft a good response. After hitting send, the popup shrank itself down to a little icon in the corner blinking "Processing."

"That should hold them, if they even have people checking it right now. Something that long should warrant a company response," Sasha smirked.

"Why the hell can the computer just ... do that?" Max asked.

"Oh. It's not normal. We can control the robots from here, but the central command can, too. They normally don't mess with us as long as we meet quota. Personal theory is that they know what we're trying to do, and they want to stop us. They can't hire scabs to keep working here. They can make sure we don't steal from them, even if it means burning a hole in their own pocket. Whole place is run by spiteful goblins who'll throw away whatever they can't sell. Same as Earth, same as Luna, same as Mars."

That made sense, in a weird, twisted, controlling way. It was "If

I can't have it, no one can," raised up to the level of businessmen and their corporate policy. Max thought, briefly, of their friends in retail who had complained about throwing away food.

"Can you disconnect this from the main system, just … lock it out completely?" Max asked.

"That's what I wanted someone here to help with," Sasha replied.

Max scrolled through looking for the offline mode option. There was one, but when they clicked on it, it cheerfully informed them that doing so would shut down all automated systems. Max puzzled over it, staring deep into the computer screen. Bit by bit, they figured out the system, intuited what it would respond to, and, with heavy use of the built-in operator's manual, they found the workaround. Or at least, they thought they found a potential workaround. It wasn't exactly a science, but if they could get admin access, delinking it from the Spire's subordination would be a few button presses away.

"Standard password shit. Your boss's name? Not like, manager. Who runs agriculture on this station?"

"Lloyd McAdam."

"His birthday?"

"Fuck if I know. Why?"

"A good 70 percent of passwords are weak as shit. They check that capital letter, special character, number bullshit sometimes, but most of them are just a name, a few letters, a special date. Hell, you know those special questions? Y'know, 'What is your mother's maiden name?' That shit can be guessed most of the time."

"So, what are you doing? Guessing?"

"Yeah. It's not exactly hard, but it is called brute-forcing for a reason. It'd be easier if I had my equipment, but I can live without it." And so, they got to typing. Guessing, looking around the room trying to figure out as much as they could. Names, cities, birthdates. Scouring the room for a physical piece. So many people—so many idiots—kept their passwords on a Post-it Note, just ripe to be taken by someone like Max, with less scruples than purpose. It was like leaving a key under the welcome mat, in that you had to assume both that everyone was on your side and that no one was smarter than you.

Two very bad assumptions to make, generally.

The password turned out to be McAdam_1. In less than two hours, they were in. The guesswork involved wasn't hard but tedious. A few lockouts, five minutes, ten minutes, fifteen minutes in turn, gave Max plenty of time to look through records. Different people were registered in the system as having different types of access—the vast, vast majority were marked as [name]-10. Sasha put forth a guess that each number corresponded, roughly, to how much control the user had over the system. And that turned out to be right. Asshole had set the password to be his username. Over six million dollars in equipment protected by laziness. Max felt a bitter glee bubble up in them, frothing and raging as they saw the admin options appear. It didn't exactly bring them pride to admit that they were going to *fucking love this.* Back when they handled stuff with the collectives, hacker groups of activist and criminal varieties, it was one of those things that made it all too fun to go through corporate systems and accounts.

As they created their new admin account, they gave it the name Fuck_You_Ashe and set its password to be as long as possible— thirty-two fucking characters. Why did they put limits on how long your password could be? Each character was a new chance for a program to fuck up, to not get it right. And each fuckup was a fraction of a second longer you had to intercept something. But, hey, they didn't make the rules. Max sat and thought. And reflected. After a few minutes, they settled on a series of alphanumerics, chosen basically at random.

"How will you remember it?" Sasha stared. "You might need to come in here again, you know."

They held up their phone and typed it into the notes program. It wasn't a perfect system, no, but remembering was a pain. At least if they kept it on something that had its own password, something they never left far from them, anyone trying to do what they had done would have a far, far harder time. They passed the phone over to Sasha, for her to enter the password into her own phone. Redundancy was always, always helpful here.

"Is there anything else you need from me?" Max asked. "Or is everything good right now?"

"I think everything's good. I'll just check to make sure that everything is working properly. Can I, uh, give you anything in return? I don't want you to leave with nothing, you know."

"Uh," they didn't really know how to respond. It'd taken a good amount of time, sure, but it wasn't really work. Not for them. Just searching and looking and making a few guesses. Getting lucky with an idiot in charge of the admin passwords. It wasn't enough for them to have earned any wage if they had been working here normally as an employee. If they had just got up, walked away and didn't get anything at all, then that'd be fair, right? It was supposed to be that way—work long enough, get something in return. You didn't get anything without work, and this wasn't work.

But that wasn't entirely true, was it? Max knew they had done something big. Or, if not big, at least not entirely pointless. They could have spent an hour, lounging around, doing nothing. Hell, they remembered intentionally stretching out how long they took to do something, just to earn precious seconds, minutes on that clock. This *was* work; this was something important. They ... had to let themselves believe that. They didn't want money, though. They couldn't take money, not from Sasha.

"Can I just have ... I don't know, a tin of strawberries? They looked pretty good."

"I saw you take some." A flush burned over Max's face as they realized they had been caught. Fuck. It wasn't a big deal—Sasha had a great big dopey smile on her face. She just leaned back in her chair, illuminated by the Hades-like light of the computer backboards. "Take as many as you want, Max."

Max left the agriculture section with a small plastic box of red strawberries, a piece of graphing paper serving as an impromptu moisture barrier. They carried the berries so carefully, like they were carrying nuggets of gold. As they went down the elevator, they didn't know how to feel. It was hard to make sense of everything. Their terror pushed to the forefront, before being grabbed and pulled back by elation, before that transformed into exhaustion and, as the floor numbers counted down, that was forcibly turned into apprehension.

This couldn't go on. The station couldn't go back to before. And they had just introduced a new variable into every equation the company would make from now on. Would they hit harder, now?

They stepped out into the food court and went to where Victoria had been originally. She was still there, sleeping on a bench. A small pillow was folded around her artificial hand. Max sat down nearby, and she stirred. Shit, did they wake her?

"Mmmax?" she mumbled as she got up. "Hey."

"You ... you don't look very comfortable, Vic."

She laughed. "No, this bench is non-sanded aluminum and spite. But, hey, my place is pretty far from here, ten floors up and hugging the outside of the sector, and I can't afford to be too far from the action."

Without thinking, Max said, "I have a couch at my place, it's not that far—one floor up and nearer to the elevators than most. You can crash there, if you want."

Victoria lit up and stood, "I'd appreciate that."

And so, they went to Max's place. There was a deep, deep unease that they felt as they punched in their password. Part of them felt, given how much people were fucking with the agriculture section, that someone would lock them out of their own home. That'd be the most convenient cruelty. But the door opened, and they entered the apartment.

Chapter Six

"You're a bit of a minimalist." Victoria entered the small apartment with a flourish, spinning around to look at it all. Max looked at the couch.

"I really can't afford to be anything else," Max sighed and leaned against the wall. "I have an extra blanket."

"It's okay," she patted her mechanical arm. "I'm just taking a nap and taking this thing off to use a blanket would just be a lot of hassle. I don't really think it's worth it." Victoria sat down on the couch. Max took a moment to think about the arms and legs and other cyberware they'd tampered with. Touted as cure-alls and fixes, as bold new expansions of human capability, they just took so much work, entire realignments of thinking. A few moments passed, awkward and quiet. "Are you feeling okay? I mean ..."

"Yeah," Max lied. "I'm fine. It's just ... I'm tired, you know? I did a lot today. The strike, the ... the fucking ..."

"It's all very overwhelming, isn't it?"

Max's face fell into their hands. "Yeah, I just. I don't know." They tried to compose themselves. Shivering, shaking, not sure how to describe it all. Emotions came flooding back in. The fear, the panic, the fact that they ran. Fuck, they felt so ashamed. The first place they'd gone was their fucking manager's officer, and how did that go? "I don't know. I don't feel cut out for a lot of the action, Victoria."

"How come? You did well enough—you helped disable the automatons."

"Yeah, and I was shaking the whole damn time. I ran when things got serious, I—"

"Do you think everyone in the station *but* you is a paragon of discipline? We're all scared. The only reason this strike's happening is because the alternative's a lot worse. Right?"

Victoria paused, let the words hang in the air. Max leaned back a little, thinking about before. Franklin's recitation of company slogans, his refusal to help. The panic that coursed through their veins when they heard the news about automation. That couldn't go on. That couldn't be their life.

Victoria changed topics. "You know, I don't really know all that much about you. Where are you from?"

"Thunder Bay," they said. "It's a town in Canada."

"Can't say I've heard of it. I'm from Prosperity, Nevada. It was an Innovation Zone, you know, a town made by the companies. It doesn't really exist anymore. Turns out a few years of summers that stay at 'kill you' temperatures will drive you out of anywhere."

"I'm sorry," Max said reflexively.

"I can't be mad about it," she shrugged. "I mean, I can be. I am. But it's not like people went quiet into that good night. Back when the electrical companies were hiking up prices and it started to become really unlivable, people planned a protest. I was about seventeen when that happened. Got into my first big actions. I mean, it was big for me. Posters and stuff, pamphleteering. Then it was January—whole town went on a general strike, refused to work."

"I guess it didn't work?" Max said.

"It did. We got some things out of it for the most part. AC was free from that point onward, and the company stopped using scrip in its last few years. A lot of people at the time said we needed to have gotten more, but it was a good first step, at least. But Prosperity shuttered up a few years later. The company had basically collapsed after we took our chance and that annihilated the jobs. I met a lot of people in the union there. The more I thought about it, the more I realized that the problem really wasn't that the company was hiking up the prices. It was that the company was allowed to and had the right to do that." She leaned back a little bit, looking up at the lazily spinning ceiling fan. "And so I'm not just here for concessions. I want the whole damn thing to change. It's not enough that they get brought to heel, bring in a new CEO and pay us a bit better. They can't be allowed to treat us like this in the first place."

There was a pregnant pause. Max didn't have thoughts to collect. Not really. It just hurt, and it hurt in a way that it never had before.

Victoria got up from the couch and walked over to Max. Put a hand on their shoulder. "Look. Bare minimum, we win the concessions from LMC that we've officially put out. You know, better wages, proper union representation. That stuff would be good, and I get why you want it. But there's a reason why it's not just us: Luna, Io, Mars, at least one of the Earth spaceports. If this goes on—goes well—it's not going to just be about the Federation here. We might be able to shift the whole damn system."

"I mean, I hope so. Maybe. But it feels so hopeless, Victoria. I just can't bring myself to think this'll go well. There's no reason to think it will. I mean, there was good stuff, we did a lot. But we're hurtling towards a wall. I can't shake off that feeling."

A weight sat beside them. Victoria shook her head, her grip steady and strong. Reassuring.

"I don't think you really believe that, Max. If it really was hopeless, you wouldn't have helped. Hopeless people don't fight back."

Max thought for a few moments. "I want to join the PFs. For real: proper member and all that," they said. "I was wrong about the corporations. I guess that was all just ... hopeful, wishful thinking on my part. And I think I want to see this all through to the end."

"Glad to have you on board," she said. "You'll be a part of PF-10 if you join with me, but you know, we're all fluid and flexible. Sometimes another PF might ask you for help, so on and so forth. There's a lot of complicated shit that goes into this, but the gist is that tomorrow, me and Joseph can propose you as a new member, vouch for you, and off we go from there."

"Thanks, Victoria," Max nodded. "I'm going to step out for a bit. Use whatever you want here. A lot of it isn't even mine, technically."

Stepping out into the hall, Max took a moment to collect themselves and wandered down to the main hall. It was an autopilot action; they often made that place their first stop on days with mercifully fewer hours or when their weekends off were actually respected. It was a big place of anonymous meeting, where you couldn't expect (and sometimes didn't want) people to learn your name. You could be alone in the crowd. A good place for contemplation.

They sat down and watched what was going on. In only a few

hours, between the time of Max ascending up to the agriculture section and now, the entire place had been transformed. People sat gathered around the stores and shops now flung open and made into kitchens or supply centers. Posters and signs hung on walls with different slogans or ideals: demands, the points of unity for the Federation a few extracted from old books and new pamphlets and blogs. "*We demand the impossible!*" was a particularly funny one to Max. There was constant, shifting, endless change.

And Max couldn't sit any longer. Even though they were tired, exhausted, hurting, they got up and offered to help. A few people were moving benches, trying to make a proper barricade with supplies most helpfully loaned from manufacturing and whatever else was around—metal chains, freshly printed and still slightly warm to the touch, with benches and tables. They didn't need to be tall, Max was told, they just needed to be present.

In and out of the maintenance tunnels, the hallways that lead from the monorail station, the transport junctions, Max helped carry benches and chairs. It was hard physical work, stuff they had done for hours upon grinding hours working at the dock, but here they felt that sense of change, of shifting in the air. It didn't really make sense to them yet, but they felt it and for some reason the work didn't suck as much now.

Somewhere along the line, they met up with Joseph, who was in that same state of enthusiastic exhaustion as Max. When the two met up, they shared a knowing nod and got to wordless work.

The barricades went up, bit by bit, bench by bench, each around waist high. Some had gates, others you just vaulted over if you really needed to get by, but all of them seemed strangely insufficient to Max. Like you'd really be able to stop a dedicated testudo of security with chained-together benches and tables and shit.

"Will this really hold them off?" Max asked.

"It doesn't need to, kid," Joseph said. He took a long, deep inhalation from a vape pen. "We measure the success in seconds and minutes. Days are good, but if a group of dedicated fuckin' pigs came barreling down on this?" He gestured to the two layers of barricade in front of the transport junction. A third was being made behind them. "The minute or so it would take them means we could get enough people here to hold them back proper. No such thing as a perfect wall; we just gotta make them fail well."

"So, if they fail well and you drive back the security, you just rebuild it," Max nodded. "Makes sense."

"That's the idea. It's a good philosophy, if you ask me. Gotta make sure you fail well. Goes for walls, computers, strikes. Strikes especially."

"What do you mean?" Max furrowed their brow.

"Oh, nothing. Just shit I've heard down the grapevine," he grinned and took another long drag. "The Martian coordinating committee resigned; the Ionians haven't picked up any of our calls after pledging support. It's like we jumped stiff-dick-first into a concrete floor after everyone else had joked about doing the same." Max had to wonder if Joseph had ever done that or if his mind just worked in mysterious ways. "I'm starting to think it'll go badly."

"Come on, don't be a pessimist," Max laughed off the negativity best they could.

"I like to set my expectations low. The world has a way of proving me right, Max. I figured it'd suck to be here. I figured it'd suck to work the docks. I figured we'd get into some real shit, and each time I got it proven right. If I'm wrong, then I'll be very pleasantly surprised."

"I don't know, I mean, I was helping out in agriculture and their systems were shit." Max leaned against the wall.

"Shit? Whaddya mean?"

"I mean that the admin password was the same as the publicly viewable admin username. Whole system's probably built to the same standards, if I had to guess."

"Hah, great. Good to hear. See, that right there, that's what I'm calling a pleasant surprise. Good job, Max," he smiled with a genuine warmth. "But still, I wouldn't put too much faith in that hypothesis."

"Why not? If that's their standard, then it's nothing but holes and exploits. We can get through all those. Who knows what their main systems are like?"

"You're not the first person to notice that sort of thing, Max. It's not that you're wrong. You're on the money, actually. It's all rickety. It's all held up by duct tape and glue and poor welds, all done by the lowest bidders. But it has staying power for a reason. It's not that these last three hundred years companies have been secretly hiding their weaknesses or anything. It's that when you build everything on the cheap, you don't spend much to rebuild it either, and every break gives them something, *something,* to make money off of." He paused, reached into his pocket and pulled out a dented hipflask. A deep swig—Max could smell the whiskey—and he offered it to them. They put their hand up in silent rejection. "Climate change? Carbon capture and advanced cooling and geoforming made sure that only *some* of Earth became uninhabitable. Collapse of agriculture? Half the countries of the world grow meat now in big ol' labs run by biotech companies. Space travel? Well, look how that turned out!" He gestured around himself at the station, letting the dim lights and concrete emphasize his point. "The ricketiness, the weakness ... it means that anything we topple gets built again because some other contractor asshole's waiting in the wings. *Three hundred* years of this," he sighed deeply. "And there's been damn good things done. Bombs thrown, windows broken, CEOs shot. But none of it worked before. They rebuilt. It all still feels like we're waiting on Christ to render judgment. Most folk stopped believing in that a while ago."

"I'm ..." Max paused, their hands balling and relaxing in turn. "You can't tell me we're not going to change anything, Joe."

"No, not nothing. Just don't get too comfortable." Joseph walked away. "Now the other PFs are gonna take this sector over. So, maybe clear out, eh?"

With nothing else to do, Max left. They couldn't think of a counterexample, a contradicting event for Joseph. Every try came up short, came up blank. Either a success that was blunted or a crushed resistance. A deep unease grew. It would calm down after some sleep—it almost always did.

Just for good measure, though, on the way back, Max passed by one of the stores-turned-depots and picked up a case of beer. It was marked down in the cash register and, almost instinctively, Max put their hand under the laser reader for the pay-pad to note and make the transfer. After a few awkward tries, the person manning the thing politely told Max that the reader had been disconnected and they could just ... walk out. The register existed just as a system of logging, tallying stock.

Max walked out, feeling even more uneasy. It was stealing, wasn't it? On the long list of things they had done to land them in jail, it was comparatively minor. But it still felt wrong, a break in how things were supposed to be done. But existential crises aside, they made it back to their apartment just fine. They opened a beer and sat down on their bed, looking around.

Victoria was napping already, her mechanical arm kept elevated and away from any potential snags. Bare plastic and metal, it should be removed before rest. But like Victoria said, that could be too much of a hassle given the circumstances. Max just hoped Victoria could actually, really rest. She deserved it.

They sighed, slipped off their hoodie and took a long swig of beer. It tasted like piss—as if they would expect anything else. As they allowed themselves a few minutes of real, proper rest, the entire day seemed to collapse onto their shoulders. It wasn't very hard to get to sleep.

Chapter Seven

Max woke up in a considerable amount of pain. Not sharp or anything, just that post-effort ache that anyone who's said "Today, I'll start exercising," is familiar with. A bleary-eyed glance at the clock told them it was 8 p.m. or thereabouts. When they shifted out of bed, they let out a long, tired groan. Their back hurt, their legs were jelly as they tried to shuffle upright. Two ibuprofen pills and a swig of instant coffee later, they felt a little better.

They sat down at their desk. There had to be news or updates or something, right? Something interesting to read. With mounting confusion, Max tried to go to any of their usual websites, from the corporate to the underground, and each one turned up as "blocked," or "server failed to connect." They squinted and tried to diagnose the problem. VPN? Didn't change a thing if it was on or off. Resetting their connection? Nope. It was all just shut down. The troubleshooter was little help, just declaring that "connectivity problems" were the cause of it all. Were they cut off? Was it just their computer?

They checked their phone to no avail. It was down, too. Even data didn't work. Signal was weak, too, but not completely down. Maybe somewhere nearby was still functioning properly. Something, someone was fucking with the station's Solarnet connection. Temporary disruption? They sighed and looked through their contacts.

"Hello?" Sasha said. Sasha worked and lived in a wholly different part of the sector. If she had something funky going on, then it was a whole-sector issue. Worth at least checking.

"Hey, Sash," Max replied. "Are you busy right now?"

"No, no, I'm glad you called. I was video calling with my boyfriend—he's in Sector C's agriculture section, y'know? And then it just cut out. Like, the Internet just stopped working."

"Yeah, that's what I was calling about," Max sighed. "I just noticed it's not working on my end. Sector's completely down, it seems."

"Any idea what's causing it?" There was a stutter, a crackle as the signal weakened a bit.

"That's what I'm trying to figure out. Sorry to bother, Sasha. I'm sure it'll be fixed soon. Bye." They hung up and tossed their phone on the bed. Thing would be useless until that's back up.

Someone stirred behind them, and Victoria let out her own tired groan. "Were you talking to someone?"

"Yeah," Max said. "Just Sasha. Uh, friend of mine, you know, in agriculture. Might've talked to them. There's something going on, Victoria. Solarnet's down for the whole sector."

"Wait, what?" Worry crossed her face. "Are we getting anything in or out?"

"I've tried. Phones still work. I mean, you can call people, but the signal's not great."

"Oh, fuck," Victoria dropped her face into her hands. She let out a long sigh, the type only given by people who had expected the worst and had still not prepared enough. "Fuck, this isn't good. Have you heard anything from the other PFs? Wait." She patted her pockets down, looking for her own phone. It was a cheap, easy-to-replace model. "Okay, uh. I just have a text reminding me about the PF meeting. Apparently they're calling it tonight. Missed calls? No messages." She moved frantically, trying to process all the information at once. Max hadn't seen her like this before, talking to herself as she worked through everything. After a few moments, she came to a conclusion. "Max, we might be completely cut off from the Solarnet. If we can't get packages through or communicate with the other affiliates, we're just floating in the dark. They could be hiring PMCs to do what security couldn't, and we'd have no way of knowing. We don't even know how they're spinning this damn thing. Counternarrative is impossible, it's all ..." She spoke quickly, stumbling over her own words. A deep breath in, then out. "The other PFs probably have an idea of what to do. We're going to go to the meeting tonight."

"When is it?"

She looked down at her phone, checking the time. "Forty-five minutes. I seem to have, uh, overslept," she admitted sheepishly.

"So did I. At least we won't be late. Do you want some coffee?"

"That'd be great," she smiled. "This is just all sorts of wrenches thrown into all sorts of gears. We were in talks with the new Martian committee to ensure continuity of plans and trying to get in touch with Ioians over all this. I hope they won't be *too* angry at our coordco for not responding in time."

"Joseph was telling me about that," Max sighed. "Troubles with the other unions?"

"Oh, I don't think it's trouble per se. It's just a lot of questions that need to be sorted out," she said. The optimism, Max could tell, was strained. "It'll be fine."

The two of them walked together to the meeting. It was being held in what used to be a general mess hall, a place where people could bring whatever they wanted and relax in the anonymity, safe under the gaze of security cameras. Those cameras had been disabled, of course, but Max could still see the holes where they had once been mounted.

Something that surprised Max was just how many PF members there were. Victoria was helpful enough to inform them that the five-dozen-and-change people gathered around the table were, in fact, only those who could come. Those who couldn't had sent regrets and trusted their friends with their vote. Max would, they figured, understand it in time. It was a bit difficult to hold a meeting in these circumstances.

"Who's this?" some guy asked Victoria, looking Max up and down.

"Don't worry," she said. "Prospective member of my PF. They're good."

"Right," he said, nodding. "I don't want there to be any sort of, you know, *incident* during this meeting. Just trying to be careful."

"Of course," Victoria smiled. "Max is no trouble at all, trust me."

There were people outside, checking to make sure that all attendees were proper union members. Transparency came at the risk of informants, and what measures they had were handshakes, trust, official membership roles and vouching for others. Someone was turned away—they needed a PF member to vouch for them—and with a stamp of their foot, they turned and walked out.

As for those who were allowed in, the PF members sat in a tight, Round Table manner—only there was no table to complete the image, and Max was fairly sure King Arthur wouldn't actually approve of this meeting. Something about that "No Gods, No Masters" poster that hung on one of the nearby pillars.

The meeting came to order. Well, order was a strange way of putting it. It proceeded with people volunteering to take various roles, recording minutes and such, and people arguing whether that was even needed right now. What good would it be to record minutes and seconds when they can't even be sent out? But eventually protocol won out. They'd need to review things later, after all. Max didn't have an opinion and just felt awkward sandwiched between Joseph (who had come late and, surprising even to himself, without a hangover) and Victoria. They could feel the eyes of other people looking. That "Oh, a new kid" look that got a "Please, don't hurt me" look back.

After the question of minutes, people started talking business. It was moderated, mediated, by someone who had volunteered for the role and did her best to stop interruptions—a tall, blonde woman who had a deep, commanding voice. Her name was Elisabeth, if all the "Sorry, Elisabeths" were to be believed.

When did the Solarnet go down for everyone? Someone said two hours ago. Another said they found out about it an hour and a half ago. Well, what was it—two hours ago, an hour and a half? Does it matter? Someone pointed out that this was something they were expecting. Another said that it wasn't something they could prepare for, just prepare to fix. All sorts of reasons, blames, veiled insults were given as people tried to worm their way around the fact that attempts to bring in Spire IT had failed, and they knew this shit would happen sooner or later. Elisabeth jutted in again, telling everyone to shut the fuck up and start problem solving. Blame was for later. The conversations rolled along, moved along in great, clunky sections. Then came the big question, two packaged into one: What happened and what do we do about it?

Victoria nudged Max.

"What?"

"You have any ideas? Come on, you should know *something*," she urged. Max thought for a moment. They didn't feel like they *could* speak yet. They weren't sure. They whispered back.

"Is it okay?"

"I'm telling you it is," Victoria replied. "Besides, it might make a good setup for what I'm going to suggest," she smirked.

"What are you planning?"

"Well," Joseph said beside them, "me and Vic were talking about this earlier. How do you feel about helpin' us all fix the Solarnet problem. I don't need to tell you how much it'd help us all out, do I?"

And there was the shot. Max just nodded assent to the idea. They didn't want to make a scene, not now. Deliberation could wait, but the answer for now was yes. They raised their hand slowly.

"Yes, you?" One of the moderators said. "Your name? I don't recognize your face." He was an older man, someone Max didn't recognize either.

"Max. I'm, uh. With Victoria. Some of you might know me," they did see a few vaguely familiar faces. "I do blackhat work in this sector. I don't know how many of you guys got experience with computers, but I think I have an idea of what happened with the Solarnet."

"Go on."

"It's not a glitch, I think we've all figured out that much. But the station has a central control for the Solarnet, so we can't fix it from here." Dozens of eyes stared at Max saying, "We know, asshole." They retreated a bit into their chair. "Sorry, thinking aloud. If I had to guess, it's probably just someone who dicked around with the settings, not anything permanent. Hell, I wouldn't be shocked if it was localized to the sectors. It'd be as easy as disconnecting whatever nodes from the server and letting the Solarnet run itself out." There was that feeling again, like back at the automatons. Of letting words and explanation tumble out. "I don't know how useful the physical wires and limited phone signal will be, but that looks like our only option."

"So," the older man said, "your official diagnosis is that we're fucked?"

"Unless we got some friends in the Spire who have access to the main Solarnet server room, we're basically isolated from the wider world. We just won't have powerful enough signals."

There was a collective disappointment. Max had crushed some of them, and they felt horrible for it. It was the truth, of course, but they saw people's faces drop and shoulders sag.

"If I may?" Victoria stood up. "I'd like to kill two birds with one stone, if you all don't mind."

No one objected.

"First of all, Max is a prospective member of PF-10. Me and Joseph are here to vouch for them," she started. "I met them properly about six days ago, but Joseph's known them since before they were on this station, so take his word over mine. But in that time, they've helped me carry out the disabling of the automatons and also helped the agriculture section deal with that little problem they had. So, I'd like to table a motion to accept them as a member of the Protection Forces."

Max felt their heart pump a little faster in their chest. God, this was it. They thought back to months ago, idly mentioning to Joseph that they wanted to help out more. Fixing people's limbs best that they could and making sure to keep their head down didn't cut it. The automation plan and the tears they cried over it. And now this, just waiting to see what happened.

Joseph was asked his testimony. Max didn't even listen to it—they were too caught in the twisting, churning gut feeling. They almost wanted to object to their own membership, say that they couldn't really help that much, something to get *out* of this.

Was Joseph telling that story about the time they smoked weed in a shipping crate? At least it got a laugh.

When it came down to it and people were asked if they'd accept Max into the PF, no one really objected. Raised concerns and questions but no one out-and-out objected. A sense of relief and renewed fear washed over Max.

"As for the second bird," Victoria said, "I'm volunteering the services of PF-10 to attempt to fix the Solarnet. It'll require infiltration of the Spire and a decent deal of preparation, but with my team being small as it is—newly three people—and with Max's skills, I'm confident we can get it up and running again."

"If they turned it off once," said someone, "what would stop them from doing it again?"

Max was given the floor once more.

"Oh, uh. Off the top of my head? I don't want to make claims or anything. I don't know if they went with physical damage, but it seems unlikely. But if they did, then there's nothing we can do. If they didn't, I could probably restore the system, maybe change passwords, restrict their own access, that sort of thing. I'm no miracle worker, but that seems doable. I don't really know if it's—"

Joseph chuckled and nudged Max. "Jesus, have some confidence in yourself. 'Maybe' this. 'I don't know' that. Christ, might as well throw in a few mea culpas."

Max nodded, took a deep breath. A few moments to collect themselves. "It's not the hardest thing once you have physical access to the computers. I can do it."

"It's worth the risk," Victoria interjected. "If we don't do something, we're stuck until we've been cleaned up and we're nothing but stories for *LMC Daily News*. This whole strike is hinging on our ability to communicate now."

It was decided. Three objections: One on the basis of expediency—it could take too long. One on the basis of resources—they might not have enough to equip a team for an excursion. One on the basis of risk—the Spire was the epicenter of the whole damn security force.

The motion still carried.

Chapter Eight

After the meeting, the PFs had to deal with conclusions and discuss with other sectors over those physical wires and connections that still functioned. The data streaming through them was fast and reached anywhere and everywhere in the station. It wasn't a problem, at least not strictly, of communication. From the different terminals and computers where fiber optics ran, one could communicate damn near seamlessly with anyone else in the station. The only problem is that it could be tapped. Communications were brief, cryptic and encrypted on top of that. As long as everyone knew what was going on, it sufficed, and the channels were shut down as soon as possible.

After the meeting, Max decided that some more sleep would be a better idea than deliberation and doubt. They had said yes, they had wanted to help. This was the end result. They could manage that, right?

Sleep was uneasy and sporadic. When they finally got up, convinced themselves to come back to the waking world, they felt even more tired than before. A different tired—numbness, really. They looked at the clock. The meeting had ended at nearly midnight; it was now somewhere around 5 a.m. Victoria had told them to meet at the barricades at the monorail around ten the next day. With so much time and nothing to do, Max wandered aimlessly. They hadn't asked if they could help or anything, it had just been a beeline back to sleep. They thought they should feel bad about that, but their brain decided anxiety and a cold, hollow feeling were suitable substitutions for guilt.

Max swallowed coffee from a small Styrofoam cup. They took a bite out of their burrito and sighed. Someone was playing music from their phone, distant and almost drowned out. Max didn't recognize the singer or the song. Some pleasant, soft chords that sounded like they had been recorded live, electronic jitters that were too consistent to be audio glitches. Half syllables, repeated again and again in the chorus. Max felt their thoughts pause and repeat with those syllables. Nothing coherent enough to express formed, and they felt the minutes and hours tick by.

Closer to the hour, Max got up and got themselves some more coffee. From the coffee machines, free of charge and with a big sign that read "Expropriated" hanging from the front, they poured a slow, steady stream of espresso. Stored in a big tank at the back, it wasn't the best in the world, but, Max reasoned, if you were drinking espresso for the flavor, then you were probably a lost cause culinarily.

The new jitters of caffeine joined the fray against exhaustion, bolstering nervous twitches and ticks. They felt their stomach rumble uncomfortably, but they bit into their burrito all the same.

They grabbed their equipment: laptop, all sorts of wires, different specialist tools of the trade, and some useful but strictly analog tools—a can of compressed air, a pocketknife (Were those still legal? They'd bought it years ago...) and a set of hex keys—all stored in their shoulder pack. With that, they slipped away from the coffee shop and to the barricade.

Coming to the barricade was the first time Max had ever seen a gun outside the hands of a cop or security guard. It was in Joseph's hand this time, a squat pistol of plastic and metal, obviously printed and given only the barest thing resembling a finish. You could practically tell the grit of sandpaper used on it.

"Wait," Max stopped, looking at the gun. "When did those come into play?"

"Security's had 'em for years. Manufacturing has the shit needed to make more. Only hard part is the bullets," he smirked. "Those need to be stolen, smuggled in or made bespoke. Not sure which one these six are. Hoping they're not made here." He made a fist over his hand and mimicked an explosion. Stupid *ka-boom* sound and everything.

"Jesus," Max said.

"Yeah, well, Vicky has one, too. I don't suppose you've ever shot one of these?"

They shook their head.

"Then don't worry about it too much. You won't be shooting one now either. Anyways, you carry the backpack. It'll have food and such for us." He gestured with the tip of the pistol to a green-and-black backpack on the ground. Max sighed.

"I already have to carry my equipment," they pointed out, patting their shoulder bag. Joseph rolled his eyes and picked up the bag himself.

"Then follow me. Victoria's waiting for us."

The monorail was down for obvious reasons and that left the tunnels. The spiderwebbing of maintenance tunnels, full of tubes and pipes carrying oxygen or fiber optic or water or any number of things that a sector needed, all centralized around the Spire's distribution networks, all automated. Max felt a lot less confident knowing they weren't really in control. Not truly. Not when there were people in the Spire that could just shut things off.

But the tunnels also led just about everywhere in the station. They were small and tight, enough for only two people to walk abreast between the pipes and cables. Max stood just outside the entrance proper, where a small set of barricades had been put up. They stepped cautiously.

"Come on, Max." Victoria offered a smile and an encouraging wave. "We don't have time to waste."

Max nodded and vaulted over the barricade. A PF who was there seeing them off bid them farewell, and the group began their march.

"So," Victoria pulled out a tablet and opened to the maintenance tunnel maps. "I downloaded these a while ago. If we were online, I'm sure we'd have more information, specific guards and stuff, but the maintenance tunnel info will have to do. If we go down route yellow," she pointed along the crisscrossed series of tubes and tunnels—it hurt Max's eyes to look at—"then we'll end up roughly around where the monorail maintenance crews work, and from there we can slip into the Spire." She gestured to the yellow strip along the wall. "That'll take about three hours of walking. Then there's a fork. Let's figure that out when we get to it."

Joseph nodded along. "You told the PFs this would take how long?"

"Three days, more or less. One to travel in, one to get to the communication sector, one to get back."

"And after three days?" Max asked.

"Consider us captured or dead," Victoria said flatly. "And then they look into sending another."

"Damn. Hope we don't take seventy-two hours and one minute," Joseph joked.

Max felt a shard of ice worm its way into their heart. They took a moment and put their back against the wall.

"You're not getting cold feet already, are you, Max?" Joseph teased. "Come on! It's just getting fucked up and possibly killed. No big deal."

Victoria groaned. "Joseph, stop."

"You gotta break the recruit in, even if they're your friend."

"Stop. Joseph, please stop," Max said. "I'm fine. I'm fine. I don't have cold feet or anything, promise. You guys can count on me," they said, more to assure themselves than anyone listening. They got up and kept going down the tunnels, trailing behind Victoria. Joseph was a fucking prick. He was a fucking prick who never grew up and never changed and just ... fuck. They had to make pleasantries, at least. Talk to the guy. Maybe the "please stop" was enough. Maybe.

"Sorry," he put up his hands defensively. "I'm just trying a little dark humor, is all."

"Okay, it's ..." Max breathed. "Sorry, let's go."

Their footsteps echoed in the harshly lit tunnel. Anyone in the system—in the spreading veins and arteries of the station—could hear them. At least it sounded that way, as heavy boots and runners plodded across the ground, hitting concrete with dull thuds. The thuds reverberated, bouncing off concrete and steel for what sounded like eternity. Max felt a temptation to shout. Just a simple "yop" or some other nonsense syllable. Just to hear the echo, see how far it went.

"Reminds me," Joseph said in a low, quiet voice, "of when you and I sat in the university tunnels. Had good talks about life."

Max sighed. "Not really the time, Joseph." The last time that had happened was the day they decided to skip an exam—the final one of the last semester they took—they had committed to dropping out.

Joseph had told them, "Why go? It doesn't matter now." And he was right. So, Max made that choice.

All of that had led them here, to this tunnel. As the water pipes sloshed and the steam pipes hummed, as they trailed behind Victoria, stared at the floor behind her and kept their head down, Max wondered if anyone here had made the right choice.

They came to that fork. Two tunnel paths crossed, one marked in yellow and the other in green. The group all sat down in a small room off to the side of the tunnels—a rest stop for engineers who did their long patrols. It was unlocked, and there was nothing really valuable within, but still, Max suspected someone had become lax with protocol. The room had a table with a few folding chairs. Bare concrete with pipes that ran refrigerant and coolant weaving across the back wall. It was strangely warm.

"I wonder how they're doing back at the sector," Max said.

"Probably pretty damn drunk on their own success right now. I just hope they're running patrols on time. I'm more interested in how the company's doing," he continued.

"Why do you care?" Max asked.

"Because I like watching them squirm," he grinned. "But it's pretty obvious. They're not negotiating; they're not looking into a way out. They're probably negotiating with Blacklune."

Blacklune. The name rung clear in Max's mind. Mercenaries for hire, who deserve to be in The Hague and then hung. Depending on who you ask, they're responsible either for *defending* themselves during the Eurydice Insurgency or *for* the Eurydice Massacre. Three hundred seventy-two workers injured, forty-seven dead, only one causality from Blacklune.

"Do you think they'd actually use them here? We're still under Earth law on the station, ri—"

"Do you think jurisdiction actually matters, Max?" Joseph interrupted. "Because it's mostly a nice lie people tell themselves so they can sleep at night, knowing they've ceded moral responsibility to some other group. 'Not my jurisdiction' is the extent of what most administrators and bureaucrats and bought-off judges care about. If LMC wants Blacklune, there'll be an overpaid lawyer tasking a bunch of underpaid employees to find justifications."

Victoria came in and sat down. Max offered her an energy drink, a striking blue-and-green can that extolled the virtues of working all through the night in black text alongside the ingredients and nutritional content.

"That's okay, I'm not that thirsty," she said. "But we do have some stuff to work out, if you don't mind me jutting into your conversation. There's two paths. Not sure which one you guys want to take."

"Whichever's fastest," Joseph said. "I want out of here."

"Problem is that puts us by security, or at least nearer to a security station than I want to be. The other route, though, is a big roundabout. It'd take a long, long time for us to get to the Spire."

"My answer's not really changing," Joseph said. "How close is the security station?"

"Two hundred meters," Victoria said.

"I don't want to risk anything we don't need to," Max said. "It doesn't seem worth it to save a few hours' time."

"Oh, it's absolutely worth it," Joseph countered. "Two hundred meters? They won't even hear us, see us. It's far away. Far as I'm concerned, even if we do run into a couple guys, it's not going to be that big a deal. Let me see the map, Vic," he held out his hand. She passed the tablet over. Joseph got to looking, scrolling through the map. "Yeah, see? There's places to hide if we hear something sketchy. Quicker *and* better, a rare combination."

"I don't want any run-ins," Max said.

"I *get* that, Max, but do you really want to spend hours crawling through here? If we take hours and need to drop and run, then that's several hours *wasted*."

"Look, that's not the point. I just don't want there to be trouble. You're armed, and I'm equipped with a lot of dubiously legal shit. We could play off as being just randos trying to get out maybe once, unless one of the guards tries to search us," Max explained.

"Yeah, but that's all just an *if*, Max. If we're gonna look at the concrete facts on the ground, the shit we can confirm: going the long way 'round just wastes time. Wasting time is the last thing we need to do."

"Do you mind if I break the stalemate?" Victoria asked.

"What's your take?" Joseph took another swig of his drink.

"It's not a strictly binary choice, to be careful and slow or risky and fast. We know what we're doing, for the most part. Joseph, if you're right about decent hiding places, then even assuming the worst comes to pass, we can probably make it out of there alright. If we're careful, we can take the fast route."

"Alright," Max said, finally assenting. "I don't know what'll happen either way. Let's go with the short route."

Joseph chugged his energy drink. It was empty in seconds. He tossed it casually into a corner of the room and stood up, offering

Max his hand. They took it. The pull upward was rough and hurt their shoulder, but they straightened out their back, felt the joints crack into place. Saying that they were ready would be a lie. But they'd be more ready than before.

And so off they went through the tunnels, following that bright yellow stripe. Max held their breath more than before, flinching at each and every sound. Every intersection and corner, they took pause. Victoria or Joseph would take point, glancing down each hall and corner, listening before they swiftly moved on. It was hard to be quiet in the halls. Steps echoed. Rubber soles squeaked. It was slow, cautious work.

The security outpost came up and an arrow of chipped paint pointed in its direction down the hall. It felt like they were walking toward a cliff. Their steps became slower still, creeping through and communicating through gesture. Go here, stand still, this and that.

Max's blood froze when they heard something down the hall. A squeaking, moving sound, pistons and rotors humming and approaching. Victoria looked back at them and motioned for them to come closer. They didn't want to, but they took the step. Victoria whispered to them.

"Autonomous patrol," she said. "Stay quiet."

Max wanted to say something along the lines of "easier said than done," but stayed quiet. They didn't know how well it could hear or even what it looked like. They pressed themselves against the wall, took short, shallow breaths. The squeaking, rubbery soles of four feet scooted across the hall. It emerged, as Max pressed themselves as hard as they could against the wall. A small cyan and black thing, the size of a Labrador, walking on ball feet with an awkward fluidity. It didn't walk like a dog, with each leg moving independently of each other in a 1-2-3-4 pattern. The head didn't move at all, resting on the folded crane it had for a neck. Max recognized it instantly: a K9, one of those damn security dogs they had.

It shifted and moved around as it walked, stopping only to swivel its head to one side or the other. It was completely autonomous, Max noted. It moved ten steps then looked, all in a set pattern of too-perfect timing. Each action had a distinct stop, start, stop. Nothing had the human touch of error.

Once the K9 had moved past, gone down the hall, Victoria just sighed.

"We should have taken it down," said Joseph. "I coulda lunged and grabbed its battery release. It's just along the stomach."

"And if you were off by an inch?" Victoria asked. "And your hands jammed themselves in the joints?"

"Okay, sure. Freak accident, sure. Is now really the time for caution, Victoria? Or do you want to actually do something?"

It rounded the corner, vanishing from sight. It had neither seen nor heard them, and the collective relief filled the air like a drug. Its effects were short, of course, and the team began moving again.

Max thought for a bit. It hurt, thinking. Like an overclocked computer, running the same process over and over ad infinitum until something crashed, broke down. They didn't know where they stood yet, but still they stepped forward, still moved. Toward the Spire, toward the epicenter of it all.

"Hey, Max," Joseph said. "Do you think I could have gotten it?"

"It wouldn't be a good idea anyways," Max said. "The K9 is autonomous, but there's still someone watching it. Probably bored, probably tired, might be on his fifth cup of coffee in as many hours. But he's watching. If the feed shut down, then he'd know something was up."

"Maybe you're right," Joseph said. "But come on, wouldn't it be fun?"

"Fun's not the object here. Aren't you scared of being caught or something?"

"Of course I am," he laughed. "You have to be scared. You'd be insane otherwise. But come now, Max. You can tell everyone that you were pulled along by insane forces, people who didn't have their right mind about them. Might get you a lighter sentence."

"Is that all you see, Joseph? A prison sentence?" Max asked.

"Call me a realist, Max. It's hubris to think we're special here, or that the cops won't catch us at all. I'm just prepared."

"Why do you do this? If you're so sure it's going to end badly, why?"

"Because I love the work. I love this," he breathed in deeply. "Look, Max, just because I'm a bit of a glass-ever-empty guy doesn't mean I don't enjoy what I'm doing. It's fun. It's the closest to an extreme sport I'll ever have. Saves me from wanting to go space-vaulting or something," he smiled humorlessly. Max thought they saw a flash of sadness, exhaustion, in his eyes. It left as soon as they noticed.

"I don't ..." Max sighed deeply. "I don't understand how you can think that. I wanted to do something that has a purpose, for once. Do you think this is pointless?"

Victoria started ascending a ladder. She vanished in seconds, climbing like a spider up, up and away. Max and Joseph made their way over.

Joseph put one hand on the ladder, looked at Max and said, "Pointless? Never said that. There is a point. It's this: it's never enough for them to have all the power, the money, the ears of prime ministers and presidents and kings. It's not enough for Ashe to have all the power in the universe. He wants to be loved by us, too. He wants to live like good King Arthur, loved and cherished and appreciated by his serfs. I like throwing a wrench into that. I think it's important. And, who knows, maybe the next set of malcontents will learn something from us. I doubt it, but there's my optimism for ya. If we don't do it, no one will. If we don't fight, then he might start thinking he's loved and cherished, eating his own bullshit. That. Can't. Happen."

And he ascended the ladder. After a few quiet seconds, Max did, too. As they climbed, they tried not to think too hard about what Joseph had said. The thoughts kept creeping into their mind, autonomous. As they moved up the ladder, they felt themselves get lighter and lighter. They didn't want this to all be for nothing, and there was a deep, sick feeling that it would be. But they had their mission, they could at least focus on that. Get to the Spire, get to the server rooms and restore the Solarnet. That, they could do. That, they had to do.

It wasn't too long, at least, before they entered the Spire. And when they did, Max's jaw dropped.

Chapter Nine

The Spire—that beating commercial heart that every sector worked to maintain—was beautiful. Seven pillars reached kilometers up and down into the sky. Silver and steel and bent plastic with stained-orange windows, hexagons running up and down in distinct, even rows. Each pillar had what looked like a dozen elevators suspended around them—moving up and down, carrying few people but never still. There was no ceiling, no hard barrier or border between each floor, just the pillars, each hundreds of meters across. Standing before them, on the tiny walkway of webbed iron and plastic, Max felt like an insect staring up at a Roman temple.

"Jesus Christ," they muttered under their breath, their eyes drawn to the central, vast column that all others were subordinate to. All covered in huge angled screens so whatever was playing on them towered over you, stared down at you, and windows facing each and every floor of every tower in some pseudo panopticon. Max had always known, of course, that the station was huge, that the Spire was huge. When the spinning of the station brought glimpses of the Spire into view, when they stood near a window that faced it, it was always dominating the view, blotting out the sun, the stars, the distant planets of Earth and Mars. But its true scale, its overwhelming enormity, only made sense when they stood there under the gaze of the towers and felt their stomach churn.

They stepped out onto the great interconnecting concourse— the bridges of concrete and marble that connected every tower to the great central column—and saw the gardens. The fountains, the carefully drone-tended flowerbeds of roses outside cafés set up in simulacra of Parisian bakeries and coffee shops. They were still manned by people dutifully fulfilling their posts. The gurgle of fountains and gentle humming of elevator counterweights was punctuated by the hiss of an espresso machine.

The lord of this domain, the smiling, phlegm-haired Mr. Ashe, appeared on the screens. The sound would have been overwhelming, coming from dozens of speakers under dozens of screens. But it was contained, directed by technology and audio fields, so that each speaker produced a cone that neither overlapped nor could be ignored. It was a single voice, emerging from dozens of mouths.

"Good evening, my LMC family. In this time of current struggle, I wish to remind you all, residents of the Spire of Station Six, that you have nothing to fear. The corporate board just signed a resolution not to negotiate with these terrorists. We are in further talks to discuss how to move forward. Those of you who are here on vacation will soon receive the codes to call the secure lines should you need to aid for any reason. The LMC Security Division is well able to help with your needs or can transfer you to one of the appropriate subdivisions. Now, on to the important news!"

His face lit up as he spoke, as something shifted. This didn't seem like a pre-recorded message. He wasn't as unbearably still as before. He emoted, changed. He smiled, then frowned a bit, then smirked sly as the devil. "Even accounting for the worst-case projections, the LMC stock has been on the rise—up three points, last I checked—which isn't the meteoric rise we all wanted, but remember that slow and steady wins the race. In addition, in terms of raw profit, our corporate family is looking at an increased quarterly profit of seventy-two billion dollars—even more once our bold Automated Future Plan is put into proper action, which I assure you, it will be." Even on the screens, in the distance, Max could hear that malice, that subtle, hateful malice. "This has been Maximilian Ashe, CEO of Lunar Module Construction—though we may rename soon, for under my tenure we have grown so much more. Signing off."

The screen flickered out and the LMC logo took over. Victoria looked up at the screen they had all been watching and spat.

"Asshole."

"I wonder if he believes the words that spill out from his own sewage pipe of a mouth," Joseph scoffed and looked off to the distance. "Fuck, Vicky. Guard's coming. Look."

Victoria's head snapped over to see. Her eyes widened and she started moving. "I saw a restroom up ahead. We can hide there for a bit."

"Seems unsanitary," Joseph joked.

"The other option is running several kilometers to get to a safehouse. We've done more than enough walking today, don't you think?" Victoria was walking away as she spoke, leaving everyone else behind to catch up.

The restroom was clean and proper. It had scented humidifiers blowing a gentle pine scent into the air, carried by atomized water.

"We should be good," Victoria said, cracking open the washroom door. She looked around and slipped out. Max followed.

Victoria looked down at her tablet once more. "There's a set of apartments that *should*," she quietly urged caution, "be empty."

"We gotta get this over with," said Joseph. "I don't wanna just sit around for a bit, wait to see if more guards show up. We could be in and out in a few hours. Security's not going to politely wait for us. Why should we give them any damn chance to regroup?" He spoke at a normal, even volume. Victoria cringed.

Victoria leaned toward Joseph. "Maybe," she whispered, "you shouldn't be so damn loud right now. We've been walking for hours. The server will still be here whenever we decide to get going again. Besides, they don't know we're coming—something they *almost* found out last time we listened to you. Ran right into security less than an hour ago, and you want to, what, keep running ahead?"

He shut up after that. Max kept glancing at him as the group walked to the nearest pillar. He was simmering, or reflecting, or something. Maybe both. The group kept pace with Victoria taking the lead. She peeked around corners and guided them across the walkways toward the nearest pillar.

Standing next to it felt almost humiliating. Everything about the architecture of the Spire, everything about its construction, made Max feel small and tiny. They weren't even worth considering next to the pillars. Each one was monolithic in its own right and seemed to cancel out anything human, anything grounded. Any reference point just vanished, staring high, high up at the glass towers. Even a comparison to a mountain fell flat. They were too artificial for that.

"Come on," Joseph grunted. "Stop gawking."

The inside of the pillar washed away Max's agoraphobic wonder. It looked normal, a hotel lobby that seemed entirely too rich for their class of person. Synthetic marble, blown glass and minimalist furniture dominated the lobby. All the chairs and tables were desperately trying to show off that they were, while just plastic, fancy, cool, sleek plastic. Not like the cheap chairs that found their place on so many scorched lawns. These were far fancier, even if they were the same material and made through the same process.

There were a few workers in the lobby—mostly people who looked too exhausted to care. The secretary at the front just looked up at them, not speaking, barely moving. Victoria walked past with the confidence of a regular, not stopping to ask anything. The group moved with her, trying their best to look like they belonged. To slip into the background.

An elevator chimed with an electric tune, and everyone stepped inside. The three walls of the elevator were mirrors. Max got a good look at their infinitely repeated self. Bags under eyes, a bruise on the side of their cheek—where had they even gotten that? Maybe one of the falls during the opening hours of the strike. God, they looked like a fucking mess. They made a mental note to fix themselves up once they got wherever the group was going. Victoria seemed to know what she was doing, where she was going, and Max trusted her well enough.

The elevator glided through its shaft quietly. They kept these a lot better than the ones in the sectors, Max noted. Of all the things to gatekeep behind finances. Oh, what tragedy it would be, if the elevators for the well-to-do and the just-visiting rumbled slightly.

Floor seventy-three was a quiet place. The first thing that Max saw was a large tank—thick, black gravel with tropical plants rooted deep, fish lazily swimming and kissing at the surface of the water as flakes fell in, shaded by a simulacra of jungle canopy. Flanking it on each side were doors to storage, then the apartments. If there were people around here, they must have been hiding away in their homes, trying to wait out the situation. A delivery drone rumbled down the hall, carrying a paper box of food inside a plexiglass container. The Spire folks still got delivery. Max wondered for a second if the whole place had been automated well before they got here. They didn't actually know, they realized.

Apartment 73-342 was empty. A digital sign on the front cheerfully informed people to contact a given phone number or email to discuss pricing options for aspiring residents. It used that specific word: *aspiring*. Was living here really someone's aspiration? Max doubted it. It would be comfortable but not much better than just living in the sectors. After Joseph picked the lock, Max stepped inside and saw what the apartment was like. It had a few rooms in it, a couch and chairs and a kitchen. Overall, quite a bit bigger than what they were used to. It was plain, white, simple to the extreme. A bookshelf, a coffee table with welcome presents.

All of the books were by Mr. Ashe or his close friends. All of them had titles like *So, You Want to Be a Trillionaire?* and *Leviathan Rising: How to Survive, Thrive, and Profit in a Changing World*. All very pretentious, and Max had no interest in reading them.

Victoria fell into the couch and let out a long sigh. "Someone needs to go on watch. It's not going to be me."

"I can go," Max said. "I'm not tired or anything." And they needed some time to gather their thoughts. They didn't want either companion prodding.

They stepped outside of the apartment and leaned against the wall. No one seemed to be coming, at least. They ran through the day in their head. It wasn't hard to work themselves up. Breathing became a conscious action, slow and steady by force.

And then they heard someone approach. From the right, there was a heavy, plodding sound of boots on the ground. Their blood turned to ice, and they pressed themselves against the wall.

"Max? The hell are you doing here?" Franklin asked. Horror and relief washed over them, and their mind raced for an appropriate lie.

"Oh, Frank, hey. Uh, yeah, so, funny thing: I saw the shit going down in the sector. I was trying to clock into work, and I—"

"You heard the evac order was issued and thought that you could sneak on the outgoing ships or something?"

"Uh," Max paused for a moment. *Yes* would implicate them, make them sound like they were trying to get out. *No* would make them just sound suspect. After a few seconds, they shrugged. "A friend invited me here until it calms down."

"Of course," Franklin replied. "I'm between jobs myself. Fucking anarchists and shit, right?" He smiled widely, falsely. "I got a new job lined up for me on Luna, though, when all of this stuff calms down. I don't think there'll be much left over for here. That's how the market works. It's like a battlefield," he kept his smile up, with the trauma of experience behind it. "Gotta adapt to new conditions. It always changes, always betrays you. Always tells you to get fucked. I get that."

"Yeah," Max scratched the back of their head. "Yeah, I'm between jobs, too. I've been eyeing a job on Io though."

"Io! Fuck me, Max, fuck me. That's dogshit. You know, I have been thinking," his eyes scanned back and forth. Followed Max. "Now, I don't ... I know I said ... I ... Okay, Max. Let's do this in the most corporate-approved way. You need a job; I need workers who know what they're doing. You and me? We can continue our working relationship." His eyes sparkled. "We can get a job that won't be automated, at least not for a few years. We can get a job that's at least more stable than this. I already got one guy with me, but I have three tickets. Wanna be ticket three?"

Max froze. The breath stopped in their throat, they couldn't breathe, they couldn't ... couldn't process. Fuck. Oh, fuck. Every possibility raced through their mind: they could get a good job, they could escape, they could be done with this. No one would need to know about their actions, about what they did. It could just be ... slipping away.

"Oh," Max rolled the option around in their mind. "I, you know, that is very, uh."

They couldn't. The words wouldn't form. "Yes" stuck in their throat, coated their tongue. They took a deep breath. "I'll need to, you know, think about it. I wouldn't want to rely on charity."

"This ain't charity, Max. This is connections," he crossed his arms, seemingly unaware of what Max was getting at. If it was charity when *they had* asked, why was it not charity now when *he* offered? "But, hey, I respect a man ... woman ... uh, person, willing to stake it on their own." His eyes narrowed a bit, trying to scan Max for something. "Of course, that's if you are staking it on your own."

"I'm doing my best, sir," they said.

"'Sir' this, 'sir' that," he mumbled. "Respect'll get you far in most places, but damn if you don't remind me of my military days." There was a glimmer of recognition in his eyes, a fond memory that he shook out with a nod. "You'll do well. *Far* is a different matter, but you'll do well. Goodbye, Max."

He walked past them. Max's eyes followed him, but he didn't look back once.

Max leaned back against the wall. They wondered, faintly, about what Franklin had been offering. Probably a nothing job where they worked suicide shifts and broke their back. Nothing more.

Chapter Ten

Max had barely slept two hours when they were woken up by movement. The shuffle around the room made them snap to attention—tiredness only set back in once they realized it was just Victoria and Joseph packing up.

"So, what's the plan?" Max rubbed the sleep from their eyes.

"We know where the server room is. You know what you're doing, right?"

They rolled their neck and stretched out their back. "I should. Solarnet's run by a relay satellite a few thousand miles out. That thing's connected to us by a computer—it's always sending information. The computer just monitors everything, makes sure it's running right and according to commands. As long as we can get there, I know what to do."

"Right, but that's another problem," Joseph said. "How do we get there? It'll be guarded, and it's just one room. We have the maps of the place, but this place ain't in the business of posting its guard's patrols or giving updates or anything. Solarnet works here, but we checked—the only shit that these guys are saying are "Everything's under control" and giving assurances to Earth folk that it's not a reason to sell stocks or worry about loved ones. Not working on either count, by the way."

Max sighed. "So, what? Do we just go and see what happens?"

"Blind looks like our only option here," Victoria said. "I don't like it, not at all, but I can promise that's exactly why they disabled the Solarnet. I haven't been able to get a message back to the sector, and they don't know what's going on with us. Even if there's someone who knows what's up here, we don't know *where* they are."

"Goddammit," Max said. They rose to their feet. "Does this place have coffee?"

"Yeah, it does. Also, a complimentary cruller and a free goody bag," Joseph gestured around the apartment. "All the things that LMC gives to its squatting customers."

"Fuck you," Max yawned. "I think I can power through."

"Doesn't sound like a good idea," Victoria offered a sympathetic smile. "At the very least, we should get something in us before we go. We still have that pack of food, right? Should be an energy drink in there."

Max rifled through the backpack, reaching for one of the lukewarm cans. Garish as ever, promising them endless, boundless, infinite energy for "late nights making moolah," its only kept promise was that of cloying caffeine with a chemical aftertaste. They downed it as fast as they could. No one commented when they crushed the can and flung it at the wall.

"Let's leave before the sugar high wears down," Joseph picked the backpack up. Victoria peeked through the door and gave the all clear. It was going to be a simple trip, at least physically. Down to the bottom of the Spire's pillars, through the tunnels that connected it to the center and then to the midpoint of that central pillar. The true midpoint. All the restaurants and shops that claimed to be "central" were three-quarters up its height. It probably sounded better, advertising-wise.

They passed through the halls and Max felt themselves get lost in the monotony of prefabricated architecture. Every one of the twenty rooms they passed had the same door, the same wall around them, the same floor in front of them. It felt like walking through an endless loop, only able to tell that they were making progress because the numbers changed. From one floor to the next, from one hall to the next, there was nothing *different*. Part of them thought this had to be the energy drink making their mind race in pointless interludes and jumpstarting half-thoughts.

Then something changed—a break in the architecture, an off-white elevator marked "MAINTENANCE" that Victoria rushed over to. She pressed the button and the group waited for it. Waiting was a new monotonous pain. Max leaned against the wall and looked up. It was strange, they could almost feel the blood sloshing inside them. They knew they shouldn't be awake right now. Neurochemical warfare made everything feel weighted and delayed.

"Meet anyone during the watch?" Joseph asked.

"Huh?"

"You were watching for an hour. Asking if you saw anything or anyone."

Max paused for a moment. They felt acid form on the back of their tongue. Must be the energy drink. Couldn't be their nerves screaming at them. They didn't want to answer this. Lying felt bad, but the prospect of Joseph interrogating them felt worse.

"No," they said. "I didn't meet anyone. It was just standing around until I went inside."

Joseph nodded, frowned. At least he accepted the answer. Probably knew it wasn't true, though. He could have had his ear up against the door listening to every word for all Max knew. Asshole.

That wasn't fair. Or, at least, Max felt it wasn't fair. They stepped into the elevator and closed their eyes. Pain pulsed across their temples. Their stomach rolled as the elevator descended.

"Everything okay?" Victoria asked.

"I'm fine," Max insisted. "So, when we get to the main hub, there'll be a computer there. I can't say with one-hundred percent certainty but I know this station runs its Solarnet through an off-site satellite, and we're just going to ... its router, I guess. I know what I'm doing; it'll just need some on-the-fly thinking. I know how this station's Solarnet works, I know how this station's computers work, I've been using them since day one. It shouldn't be too hard to figure out."

"How do we deal with security, then? Since I've been told off for brushing within a few dozen yards of them, what happens when you do the same?"

"Reroute, lie, make shit up," Victoria said. "We can do this, Joseph. We've done this before. We've had worse run-ins before."

Joseph's shoulders dropped. "Okay, look, I'm just ... there *will* be trouble. I want this done quick so we have as little chance to meet trouble as possible."

The maintenance elevator gave way to the innards of the station. Solid black walls that reflected the red light from emitting tape pasted to the top corners, the lights on the ceiling all shut off, and the air near static save for a draft of cold air low to the floor where helium-coolant pipes leeched the warmth from the air. There was movement in the tunnels—Max could hear the far-off sounds of a cleaning robot vacuuming. Their steps echoed in the halls as they started to walk. They reached into their backpack, fumbling around for their flashlight. It was a small, pen-sized tube of silver, designed to illuminate the fine detail of computer hard drives, not hallways. The click was comforting, though, and the weak light made Max feel strangely better.

In any case, it illuminated the signs on the walls, direction arrows pointing here and there to elevators and storage closets and the server room. Right. The group followed the signs, listening and shuffling quietly. They moved slow, Max kept a hand out, tracing out the path on the smooth wall. They thought back to the story of the minotaur, the vast and confusing labyrinth. It wasn't a comforting thought.

Every sound sent a shiver through them. Cold sweat beaded on their forehead, their palms, their back. The fabric of their shirt clung to their skin. Heat and cold passed in waves. The slow creep kept nagging, chewing at them. After a few minutes, the sounds all started to feel like threats. Even the bootsteps behind them were disquieting—what if someone heard them? What if someone was *listening?*

Who knew what sort of taps, wires, microphones were picking up every shaky exhalation and scuff of a sole against the floor? Stuck in a recursive loop of worrying, stepping, worrying, stepping, Max trudged along. To the left, down the hall. Keep walking. *You'll make it,* they repeated over and over again. *You'll make it.*

Something was walking in another hall. Joseph's heavy hand gripped Max on the shoulder, stopping them in their tracks like a cat picked up by the scruff. Everyone waited in silence. Boots, heavy and loud and without a care in the world, plodding across the hall. Max curled their fingers, scratching their wet, itchy palms. A finger pressing slowly on the flashlight's button. Would it give them away if they turned it off? Had the light already tipped someone off?

It clicked off. No response, no change from the steps. Then a voice broke through the silence.

"Mac," said the voice, "I'm going to take a piss. Watch after the K9, will ya?"

"You took a piss five minutes ago," replied another, deeper voice. "I'm taking the K9 on patrol. Don't expect me to be around when you get back."

Another set of steps, growing further and further away. Joseph slowly released his grasp on Max. They could hear him moving behind them, standing up straighter. After a moment, he stepped forward, peering around the corner. Slowly, carefully, moving centimeter by centimeter until he was barely, barely looking.

"Clear," he whispered.

And so, they progressed. Max followed the arrows almost obsessively, trying to chart a mental path and get to the server room as quickly as possible. They figured they were close by the lights. They were on in this section of the tunnel, leaving more than just thin strips of red tape and a small flashlight to see by. The lack of guards put them on edge—they kept looking upward for cameras, for some indication that they were being watched, tracked.

That damned robot dog, that K9, was wandering the halls. They could hear it without its handler. Or maybe it was a different one? Hard to tell. But Joseph and Victoria heard it, too: the scuffing of plastic balls against the hard floor, the unmistakable sound of mechanical joints. It was coming from the exact hall they needed to go down.

Max stepped back. They tried to control their breath, shallow and rapid and loud. These things could hear, right? They had microphones. Probably more sensitive than any ear. Victoria rolled her shoulders and felt the joint of her arm. Adjusting it, maybe. Max couldn't tell.

"It'll find us. We can't let it chase us. Distract it, Joe," she said. Joseph rolled his eyes and looked over at Max. His wordless expression communicated a mix of worry, exasperation and a smug, triumphant *I told you so.*

"On it." He knelt down, like a racer about to sprint. "Give the word."

There was no word. As the K9 crossed their path, Victoria gave a gentle kick against his sole. He broke out into a sprint, darting across the halls. The K9 turned its swivel-head to look at the commotion, its entire body swaying awkwardly. She jumped into action then, wrapping her mechanical arm around the waist of the K9, bringing it down, pressing it between her arm, her stomach and the floor. Its legs kicked uselessly in the air as she reached for its battery, a cube with a visible, bright switch to pull and release. A click, a pop, and a clatter as the battery was flung across the floor. The kicking legs stopped, curling up into an idle pose. Victoria let go and got up.

"Fucking shit-hell ... fuck! You okay, Joseph?" She asked, looking down the dark hall.

" 'course I am. What's wrong?"

"It fucking pinched me," she said, lifting up her shirt and pointing to a rapidly forming blood blister on her stomach. It was about the size of Max's palm. "Bet the assholes designed it to do that."

"Fucking told you there'd be trouble. Be glad you didn't get hit with that," Joseph kicked the swivel-head. Only then did Max notice the taser under its camera, exposed like the fangs of a snake. "They know we're here now. Let's get moving."

Max burned as the group continued down the hall. They hadn't seen someone take down a K9 before—it seemed too easy, too dangerous. One wrong move and instead of a bit of adipose, fingers, feet, wrists would be going crunch between those joints. They felt their hand, making a personal promise to not even try that shit.

The group moved quickly through the hall, animated by the knowledge they had just revealed their location to the whole of the security force. Max tried to swallow back the bile.

The server room was unassuming and basic, a black-tinted glass door with an electronic lock and etched label telling the world what it was. Joseph tried the lock, jiggling the handle of the door uselessly.

Victoria stepped up and took a look at it, narrowing her eyes. "Looks basic," she said. "More of a deterrent than a preventive. I think we use the same lock on the hazardous chemical storage at work. Cracked those a million times. Anyone got a magnet?"

Max checked their backpack for a second. If they had a neodymium magnet, it would be surprising but not shocking. So many hacking methods involved just wiring yourself up to a machine directly, getting into the hardware without any need for software. But digging past the can of compressed air, the multitools, the screwdriver set, there was nothing.

"I got multitools but no magnet," Max said.

"I'll take one of those, then. Good enough."

She got to work dissembling the electronic lock, prying it off the wall directly. It was a hack job, jiggling a knife between open gaps, ripping it off the wall. But once it was on the floor, everything else opened. The failsafe made a satisfying metallic clunk, as it opened the lock in the absence of an electrical signal.

The server room was oddly cold, the coolant pipes working full time alongside the fans to keep it as cool as possible. The computers here all ran at full capacity, filling the room with white noise and drafts. Max had been in places like these before, where far more care was given to the computers than to anyone working with them. The group had to go single file between the server boards and towers of computation. Max could swear they could see their breath sometimes. They pulled their hood up and tightened the neck straps.

The main terminal wasn't hard to find, a single screen next to a desktop and a ratty chair. Every manner of cable and wire stretched out from it like the roots of an overgrown tree, tangled and disorganized and life-giving. They sat down at the chair and stared at the screen. A few shuffles of the mouse and they were brought to a login screen. *Fuck.* They had hoped that at the very least someone would have been dumb enough to forget to log out.

Brute force was out of the question. Even if they had information or something that could be used to guess, narrowing down the quadrillions of possibilities into millions, into thousands would be impossible, not within their timeframe. They didn't have time. They didn't have time for *any* of their usual routes. A few ideas ran through their head, each rejected in turn.

"Everything okay, Max?" Victoria asked

"I'm thinking," they replied.

"You don't have time to think, Max!" Joseph snapped.

"I know!" Max snapped back. "I just ... Fuck! I can't get into this computer, not with what I have, not with what we need to do. If I can't log in, I can't get *anything,* okay? I mean, even if I wire up my laptop, it'll be twenty, thirty minutes of wading through ..." they paused for a moment, their body shivering. Shivering.

Data on the RAM, encryption codes, access keys—that shit didn't decay quickly when it was cold. At their core, computers were physical processes. Cold slowed down information degradation. And the access codes to the Solarnet—the computer had to be running those programs in the background all the time, communicating and confirming messages and ensuring each package had the right keys. Three words ran through Max's head: *cold boot attack*. They pulled forward the terminal's desktop and reached for their multitools, disassembling the computer quickly. It still ran as its insides were exposed, but Max got to work setting up their laptop beside it, grabbing their external RAM drive and plugging it in. The canned air was the tool they needed. A quick test on their palm, excitement as the viciously cold air rolled across their shaking hand. They wiped their hands down—for lack of latex gloves, this was the best they could do.

They reached into the warm guts of the computer and, one by one, sprayed the RAM sticks until they went nearly white with chill. Carefully extracting each stick, holding them by the very corner tips and plugging them into their external drive, Max disemboweled the desktop. On their own computer, they started searching through the RAM, trying to find the exact pieces they needed: last used access date, password, the access codes for the Solarnet, all of it. With some help from search AI and some manual guesswork, it wasn't long until it all revealed itself to them. With the Solarnet admin access code saved as text on their computer, they turned back to the terminal. They looked at the mess of cables and wires—was Solarnet run through a program on the terminal or just through these wires? There had to be an access point on their laptop; they used the damn Solarnet after all.

A quick trip to their laptop's settings confirmed it. There was an access point, an admin code to be input. They typed it out, slowly, deliberately, double checking. They didn't want to rely on the grace of a program to not lock itself down. After a tense second, they were allowed access. The panel was resplendent with information and barren of user appeal. Simple light gray with black text detailing information packages by the number of millions of megabytes processed every second (jumping from 1.2 to 1.5), and finally, the administrative center.

Reset access code? (Warning! This will log out all other terminals with admin access!)

They wrote down their new code and saved it, copied it to the field and set it.

Max watched the program buffer and stall as the information was sent out across the station. The hand grabbing them by the shoulder came out of nowhere, sent a shock through their body.

"We have to go. Now," Victoria said. "There's people moving outside. Joseph, check for an exit. Any exit."

Max double checked everything and closed their laptop. The world came back into focus for them. People were shouting outside the server room, demanding that whoever was in there get out. The voices were loud, melding together. Three, maybe four people, all shouting at the same time. Joseph shouted in turn from somewhere across the server room.

"Here!" he said. "There's a back door here!"

Max and Victoria rushed toward the back door. A glimpse of a black-clad security guard was more than enough to send Max into a full, blind panic. As they pushed their way through the server room, they heard the crash behind them. Boot going through glass. The mechanical squeal of a K9's joints.

Joseph held the door open for them, waving them through to the halls. From there, Max followed. Down the hall, through the corridor, around the corner. There was sound behind them, shuffling and boots and more. Their lungs burned, their legs ached, they kept moving. Running blind, just trying to get far enough away that they could be *safe*.

Someone grabbed them and pulled them into another hall, down another path. They came to a dead end. Victoria was messing with something. Joseph was staring down the hall they came. Max's head darted around, trying to get their bearings. Each breath was a struggle to pull. They felt themselves collapse forward, falling against the wall.

"Come on, you fuck," Joseph growled, pulling them by the hoodie into an upright position. "I'm not letting you be a martyr."

They heard the clattering of metal and looked behind them. A ladder had collapsed down from the ceiling, leading to an upper level. They forced themselves upward. Their arms felt like jelly, their legs like lead, and each step up threatened to break them. They threw themselves over the last step of the ladder, onto the cold marble floor of an elevator lobby.

They looked up at the brightly lit signs of the lobby. Floor B5, Spire: South Observation Deck. They got up, stumbling a little as they found their footing. After a moment, they heard noise.

"What now?" Joseph looked over to Victoria.

People were moving from every direction; they could hear the sound of K9s and people and drones. From the front, directly above the now-empty secretary's desk, a small quadcopter hovered in the air. It had a large camera eye, translucent and blue, and Max could feel it staring into them. There was a person on the other side, watching them. Even if Max couldn't see them, they just *knew* they were being watched.

The elevator opened for them, and they rushed inside. It was only too late that Max saw the security guard turn the corner and raise his gun, aiming between the closing door's panels.

Chapter Eleven

Joseph collapsed on top of Max. Together, they fell, and his limp body rolled off them and on to the ground. A warm, salty *something* fell on Max's lips. Their ears rung, a tinny screech clawing on their eardrums. Someone else was speaking, but Max didn't process it. It was background, their mind too filled with other sensations. The words just rolled around in their head until they were jumbled beyond recognition.

They sat themselves upright, wiping the salt off their lips. Red streaks painted across their hands, but they refused to give a name to the red. The body behind them shifted a bit. An arm pushed the body to the side and a mouth gasped for air. Joseph was alive but from his shoulder, a thick, almost night-black fluid poured.

"—me! Jesus fucking *Christ*, Max, help me!" Victoria's strained voice screamed. Max shook their head and tried to hear past the ringing.

Joseph's shirt was in the way. It was torn most of the way open, and Victoria plunged a thick tube directly into the wound. Joseph screamed when the tube pressed through. Victoria growled something about hitting bone but pressed the button on the back of the tube. After a second, she pulled the tube out. In the wound, Max could see red-stained things ... growing, expanding. Small sponges, each coated in hemostatic and painkilling powders, swelled to expand into each torn artery and shredded muscle.

Covered in cold sweat and hot blood, Joseph was completely unresponsive, breathing in and out with shallow, rapid gasps.

Max looked around. Behind them there was a shattered mirror, a thousand small pieces held together by friction and glue; above them were harsh lights that seemed far, far too bright, and then the panel. It looked like Victoria had just raked her fingers across the buttons, hitting floors at random. Most of them were high up, eighty floors up or more. At the very top, though, Max noticed that the *penthouse* button, isolated above all others, was glowing.

The elevator door opened. It was quiet outside on that floor. It was civilian, empty. Only cleaning robots made any noise. Victoria pressed the close button, and they kept ascending.

It was four minutes before they got to the penthouse floor. They stopped gently and smoothly, and the elevator door slid open. Outside, there were a lot of apartments—directly in front of the elevator's entrance was a large wall of darkened glass, with silver etching beside the door. The etching read *"Mr. Maximillian Ashe—CEO, Lunar Marvels Construction."*

"Oh, shit," Max whispered. "This is Mr. Ashe's place."

"Not just his," Victoria grunted as she lifted Joseph upright. Max stepped in to help, pulling him up. "Penthouses for all his friends and business partners."

A quick scan around confirmed it. *Astral Mining Consortium, Ares Cybernetics,* all the great monopolies were represented here, each one in tight competition with the others for the coveted spots of "Richest CEO" and "Safest Investment." LMC might be falling a few steps behind after all this. The penthouses, too, were in a modular format, distinguished only by the names beside the doors.

Lightheadedness overtook Max. Reality itself seemed to blur and unfocus, the weight of where they were throwing them off. They stumbled a bit toward a secretary's desk situated right in front of Mr. Ashe's apartment. Their hands gripped the front edge of an ebony and marble table that probably cost more than they did. They looked down at the intricately machined metal desk toy that bobbed up and down into a crystal glass of water and took deep, long breaths.

At the desk, there was a still-active computer, its screen lighting up when Max shifted past its 360-degree camera. Motion activated. They wondered who might be watching. Probably didn't matter at this point, they were fucked.

"Door, open, now." Victoria demanded, carrying Joseph's weight best she could.

A quick look over the secretary's computer was all Max needed. One button press, and the lock on Mr. Ashe's door buzzed. A little static shock jumped from the handle to Max's hand, and they hesitated for a moment. They didn't know why but it felt wrong to be here. Being watched, for certain. That alone was reason enough to feel uneasy. But as they curled their fingers around the cold metal handle, they felt the crushing weight of *who* this was.

They opened the door. Inside was a minimalist, almost empty space. In the center was a great, suspended model of the solar system, each LMC station the size of a fist, each planet only barely larger. It rotated silently from its mounting on a chandelier. Below it were two semi-circular couches around a set of holographic projectors. As Max stepped in and looked around, the scale of it really sank in. It was a studio-style apartment, like theirs, but everything was so much bigger. They looked to the left and saw a full kitchen with a walk-in refrigerator, glasses and cabinets of real wood and etched glass. To the right, a whole set of tables and chairs, with perfectly set dishes. The entire place felt oddly empty, so much white space and unfilled floor. No pillars, supports, corners. It was an entire semi-circle that was *utterly* empty.

Then Max noticed the outlines. On the wooden floor, metal outlines of things appeared from time to time, in the vague suggestion of furniture. One was right by the door. Max tapped it with their foot. It pressed down and pushed upward, a coat rack rising up and unfolding itself. Max stepped deeper into the apartment, letting Victoria through.

Joseph was laid down on one of the couches. Victoria wandered over to the kitchen, washing her hands and wiping her face with a towel. For their part, Max took off their hoodie—noting with revulsion that some of their sick clung to the front—and hung it up.

A pneumatic, metallic sound of heels clacking down stone floor caught Max's attention. They turned around and saw her—them? It. It was an it. An impossibly slender, tall being clad in a perfect white uniform, neatly pressed and stewardess-like, with exactly as much metal and plastic needed to cover electronics and nothing more—exposed pipes and pistons moved like tendons as it tilted its head. Its voice was feminine, sweet, with the most metallic edge. Max had seen robots like it but never activated; fluttering around the edge between humanoid and art piece. Its metal eyebrows rose as it spoke; its arms, which looked like a skeleton flensed of flesh, were folded neatly in front of its torso.

"Mr. Ashe is not in right now. I can locate an appropriate time for you to meet with him."

"Oh, he's expecting us," Max said without thinking. It was just an automatic response, the first thing that came to mind.

"Ah. I am certain he will arrive soon. Mr. Ashe left 47.23 hours ago. Mr. Ashe typically returns 1.12 hours after departure. Mr. Ashe will be here soon; his absence is unorthodox. Please, guests, seat yourself. Please, guests, correct your companion's posture. Mr. Ashe does not like unorthodox seating arrangements." Its head turned, too quick to be human, to be anything but machine and lifeless silicon, to face Joseph. "Please do not lay on the couches. Mr. Ashe does not like unorthodox seating arrangements."

Victoria walked over, eyeing down the robot. Her eyes followed it. "Max, you ever seen one of these robots before?"

"Plenty. They're just in boxes most of the time," they replied. "I think it's just, like, a service bot or something like that."

Its head moved to scan Max. "I am a service automaton, Delta P-9 Endoskeleton model. I am capable of rendering nine-thousand common tasks encompassing food preparation, laundry service and basic aesthetic maintenan—"

"Medical care, can you get us that?" Victoria interjected.

"Contact with emergency services is currently disabled. Contact maintenance personnel for more detail. Please rest on the couches and await Mr. Ashe's return."

Victoria sighed. "Fuck," she said, looking at Max. "Fucking hell. Fuck." That's all she needed to say, pacing around the room, trying to think. Max stayed still, holding themselves, their mind racing. And then Victoria took a look at them, squinted her eyes and gasped.

"Max, you're hurt, too."

As if summoned by its being pointed out, there was a pain in Max's arm. The adrenaline had died down, the fear had faded, and all that was left was a painful, deep throbbing in their arm. A sickly gash of adipose dotted with blood, a flap of skin tangled in the threads. It hurt them to look at, sickened them. Pressing around the wound didn't hurt—the whole thing just felt numb, but their arm ... their arm ached. The two of them sat down on the couch as that robot had endlessly requested and got to work.

They were, they realized, strangely calm about the wound. It was like a switch had flipped in their head—*Oh, that's bad; I should fix that,* was the main thought that ran through their head. All the parts of their brain related to panic, to fear seemed to have been short-circuited, overused, stressed too far. *Oh, that's bad.* And so, they daubed on the antiseptic cream and applied a large flat adhesive bandage. It would have to do.

"How about you?" Max asked.

Victoria felt her arms, her legs. Nothing, she nodded. Nothing, except the fragment of glass that had caught her in the arm—crushed between motors and joints into sand by this point. It was a miracle, and they were glad, Max tried to express, but it came out more as a fumbled mix of "Thank god" and "Oh fuck."

The robot kept urging them to upright their companion. Max told it to shut the fuck up. It responded by requesting again. Each request grated at them, ground against them like a stone. That fucking mechanical voice, that fucking stilted speech, that ... everything, everything about it just drove deeper, harder into Max's psyche, worming its way in, in a manner they didn't think was possible.

"Can you shut the fuck up?!" Max snapped at it. "Jesus fucking Christ, didn't they install some sort of 'Take a fucking hint' program!?' Leave me the fuck alone. Don't say a single fucking thing!"

"Mr. Ashe does not like his—"

"Fuck Mr. Ashe!" Max realized they were ranting to a robot, but that didn't matter right now. It couldn't matter right now. "Fuck him, this whole entire station! Jesus Christ, can't you see the goddamn dying person!? If you have enough silicon up in that skull to see he's a person, don't you notice all the blood, too?!"

"I am not programmed for medical intervention."

Max threw the tube of antiseptic gel at it. "No fucking shit. Go away. Fuck me, I'm ..." they didn't finish the sentence. Not out loud at least. They were a failure. They were a goddamn failure who didn't know what they were doing, and they had gotten someone killed. Well, not killed. They could see his chest rising slowly, and the bleeding had stopped. However, much blood had been lost. Max sort of had their doubts about Joseph running out of here soon.

Maybe, just maybe, they could go for some sort of rescue mission? Request help? Who knew. They might need to wait it out, just ... fucking wait it all out. But, of course, that was impossible, too. Max felt the twist in their gut, the idea of sitting here, accosted by some fucking robot for days, just waiting to be found by the first person who could rub two braincells together. Nothing, absolutely fucking nothing, felt like a good option right now. Nothing felt real, even. It was a mist, a haze where the next ten minutes were unknown, and the next hour made as much sense to think about as the next day and the next week and next month.

Neither Victoria nor Max had anything to say to each other. They sat a cushion apart, letting the minutes tick by. Every few minutes, as though run by automated clock, the robot would request that they move their companion. It was a constant, unending repetition, marking the time better than any alarm could.

Please upright your companion on the couch.
Please upright your companion on the couch.
Please upright your companion on the couch.
Mr. Ashe will be here shortly.
Mr. Ashe will be here shortly.
Mr. Ash—

Max had enough of it and strode over to the kitchen table. It was surrounded by stools, hollow steel pipes holding up some godawful fancy material inlaid with who knows what. It hurt to flex their muscles; it ached to move their arms. But they raised the stool up into the air and swung hard. Pipe crunched against hydraulic, ceramic shattered, and the robot fell to the ground. It didn't get back up. It was a glass butterfly, like so much else here.

The coffee table, suspended by tensegrity wires, the thin panels of glass that separated the office space from the secretaries, everything—it was all thin. It was all fucking paper. They lived in a goddamn station that was only kept alive because of that thin wire that held it to Earth. Those shipments, the workers, everything that it needed, it imported. It was all thin, thin, thin. All that stopped that illusion from being so crystal clear here were the guards, the fucking foot soldiers who made sure that Max couldn't just break shit.

But there were no guards here, and so they swung the stool into the robot again. It was cathartic, the crunch and splintering, the force vibrating through their hands, the pain shooting through their body. It felt real.

They didn't notice the tears streaming from their eyes until the stool was broken, until the robot was a mess of leaking coolant and oil. They dropped the remains of the weapon on the ground and fell down with it.

Silence, bitter and blessed, subsumed the room entirely. No one said anything. No one uttered a sound. Nothing outside Max's ragged, tired breathing.

Joseph seemed to be doing better, bit by bit. The couch seemed practically soaked with blood, but at least the wounds themselves had stanched. His body was covered with cold sweat, staining his shirt wherever it hadn't sopped up blood. But he was breathing and better than before.

"I'm sorry," Max finally said. Their voice was a low croak, barely audible over the ambient sound of ventilation. "I could have been faster. It's ..."

"Max, you—Why?" Victoria cocked her head.

"Why was I slow? I don't know," Max said. "I don't know, I guess I didn't plan enough. I thought I knew the systems. And I should have, I mean, it was obvious. It was so *obvious* when I was there, but I just thought if I could wing it, we'd have enough time and that it couldn't be that hard. I was wrong, and now look!" They let out a sigh. "I don't know what I'm doing, Joseph kept pestering me. Maybe he's right, I was scared. I fumbled. Now look."

"I think he knows damn well the risk he took. Don't blame yourself. You didn't pull a trigger," Victoria said. "You think that just because it didn't go perfectly, it's all your fault?"

"No, it's just. Yes, sure. It's all my fucking fault. I don't know. It all sort of hinged on me, right? The goddamn *cybersurgeon* or whatever," they felt their chest constrict. The words got louder, harder to spit out. "Ever heard of a surgeon who doesn't have a plan for cutting people up? God, I'm—"

"Fine," Victoria put her hand up. "You want to give yourself a list of reasons why you're incompetent? Go ahead, Max. Go ahead. I'm not going to stop you, but don't try to rope me into it," her voice dropped a bit. "You think I haven't been thinking about it, too? About the rush to get out, the K9, everything? I'm tired, Max. I want to be back at the sector. But part of this job is dealing with consequences *when the job is done*. We can't afford to get caught up in that *now*. Keep moving. When we're done, we'll talk."

"Victoria, we're not moving. We're sitting on a couch hoping our friend doesn't go into shock. How are you able to not think about it?!"

"I just *don't*, Max. I just don't. I keep moving, I keep doing, I keep my mind off of it. Before you spoke up, I was thinking about how I would report this to the other PF teams. I was trying to come up with the exact wording." She paused to clear her throat, rub her eyes. "I was thinking about what to ask the artists to create for agitprop, and I was thinking about going to the Screwdriver and making sure Joseph got as many free drinks out of this as possible. Anything but what just happened."

"You thought at all about how we're going to get him out of here?"

"Yeah," she said coldly. "I have. We're in the central Spire, there's security looking everywhere for us, and they'll probably come busting down the penthouse sooner or later. If we head out sooner, the upper floors will probably be clear. If they're searching, they're searching for us floor by floor. Function of manpower and such.

"Far as I can tell, and for the record my experience begins and ends with protest medic training, he's not in deep shock or anything. If he's out, it's not permanent, and he won't be passing out any time soon. Probably concussed. We wait, he should be able to wake up and move around himself." She cleared her throat. "He'll slow us down, but there's no way we're abandoning him. We're aiming for the rail lines."

Max nodded along. "Why the rail lines?"

"The trains are the faster way in or out. In, they weren't viable: too obvious. We at least managed to get the drop on them. That doesn't matter anymore."

"What if we meet security?"

"I don't think I need to answer that, Max." Her voice was low and grim. Max nodded too. They couldn't afford another fuckup. Arrested, sent back to Earth, that laptop confiscated. Enough evidence on that alone to put them away for years, on top of the strike and everything else.

"Is there anything here to drink? I need something to calm down," Max chuckled. Victoria smiled.

"Not a bad idea." Victoria took a brief look through the kitchen and found the liquor cabinet.

Max was never one for whiskey. They instinctively asked for it *"on the rocks,"* hoping that it sounded fancy or something. Victoria got out two glasses, shapely and curved—she knew what she was up to, using her mechanical hand to crack the ice without any effort, packing it firm into a glass and pouring just a splash of the amber fluid into it.

"This sip's more expensive than my arm," she said. Max noted the smile, but they weren't sure if it was a joke. "Enjoy it however you want—smell it, swallow it, *skál* it. Not like I'm paying, after all."

Max hated it but drank it all down anyway. It was bitter and sharp and cold. Every sort of thing they hated in a drink, as it wormed its way down their throat. They wanted another.

Victoria smiled. "You know," she murmured, "I always thought that this stuff was more special than it seems."

"I don't know," Max looked down at their cup. "I've found that life is full of diminishing returns. I've had coffee from those instant packs I buy. I've had coffee specially grown in Florida and roasted same day, put through non-reactive filter drip ... and I can't taste much of a difference. I guess I just don't get perfection. A lot of my code's been spaghetti, and ..."

"You manage?"

"I've managed, yeah. At least so far."

There was a stirring behind them. Max jolted around and saw Joseph getting up. He groaned and spat and swore, putting his hand on the back of his head, feeling for injury.

"The fuck are we?" He asked.

"Alive, for one," Victoria said. "And stuck in the penthouse apartments, for two."

"Fuckin' hell, top of the Spire? Jesus Christ, my head ... "

"You did smash your head against a wall," Victoria said. "I'm surprised you're not worse off. And, you know, glad that you're not worse off. I'm sure there's something for pain if you look around, but me and Max were waiting for you to get up. We need to get back to sector."

"Don't mean to rush you," Max added quietly.

"Last thing I remember," Joseph said, "is getting in the elevator. Given I can *feel the holes in me,* I'm guessing it didn't go great after that. Are the rest of you okay?"

"I got dinged," Max said. "Nothing severe. Just a scratch."

"Dinged," Joseph repeated. "Dinged. Right. Let me try to ..."

He strained and struggled, using his good arm to push himself upward. Max sprung up and rushed over, offering to help him up. He pushed them away, preferring to struggle and grunt and flop his way upright. Once he was up, though, he stumbled. Max caught him.

"Fuck," he spat. "I'm fine, I'm fine."

Max let go and stepped back. He didn't look fine—his eyes darted around wildly, pale skin covered in sweat, his motions were unsteady. He moved like a tree in the wind, bending and twisting, about to fall.

He looked around for a moment, down at the smashed robot, around at the room. "Right, I'm not going to ask. Let's just go."

Chapter Twelve

Max wasn't exactly proud of the fact they had a bottle of whiskey rattling around in their backpack. Before they left, there was a brief discussion on if they should stock up. The whiskey was the only thing they really felt like taking with them—a look into the pantries and fridge showed almost nothing pre-prepared. Max caught a glimpse, in fact, of long, prehistoric-looking gray fish, their gills still opening and closing slowly, suspended in some bag of thick gel. These were labeled "Caviar."

Victoria took point. Each penthouse apartment was the same, opaque glass and doors arranged in a perfect clockface pattern. Max noticed the numbers in front of each door—Ashe was twelve; eleven was owned by some CEO who worked in asteroid mining; ten by someone who did cyberware. They didn't pay attention to the names but kept looking, trying to find some exit. Surely the penthouse had some corner hidden away for people to work on electricity and pipes and pumps.

"The elevator," Max sighed after the first walk around. "Maybe we should check the elevator. I'm sure there's a maintenance access point there."

"Do you really think I can use a damn ladder right now?" Joseph spat.

"You won't have much of a choice," Max snapped. "Unless you want to stumble through the main halls in sight of every cop and K9 and drone they have in the station."

"Jesus, Max," he grumbled. "You don't need to get on my ass."

Max caught themselves before their venomous reply could come out and sighed.

Victoria, focused on too many other things to listen in, interrupted. "We should go down a few floors. I'm sure we can find a good access point there. Looks like they don't really like having *the blue-collar types* up here. Can't see anywhere to reach maintenance or even get behind a thermostat unit."

They went down ten floors at first, to eighty-one. It was quiet there, smelled sterile and clean and vaguely chemical. Plain white panels and plain red carpeting, gold inlay and filigree (who knew if it was real), the whole place put Max on a vaguely uneasy footing. It was a parody of living spaces. Even back at the sector, as much as Max hated it, as much as they might complain and bitch, at least they knew there were other people around. Whoever used to live here must have fled with Ashe and the rest, filing into the space port when things looked even a little hairy.

They all passed by a window, one that overlooked the Spire's many pillars and towers. From this vantage point, through the translucent orange glass, they could see it. Marked with a big painted letter over the rail station, there was Sector A. It looked locked down, like a military checkpoint—they could see the men down there, scurrying like ants, the quadcopters hovering in the air.

"Don't worry," said Victoria. "We'll be fine. They'll be concentrated on the mid and lower levels. See that rail there?" She pointed to an elevated rail, one that hung in the air above everything. It followed a magnetic set of cables and constructs, loops that slid into and out of every sector, emerging out of the tunnels only around the Spire. Max thought back to before, that sense of awe and grandiosity when they'd stepped into the Spire. How much more powerful would it have been if they had been on a train, flying past pillars and docking at stations? "We can use that, if everything goes right."

"Of course," Joseph said. "I'm sure that'll be *extremely* inconspicuous and absolutely not a problem for anyone down there! Just borrow it and be on our way!"

"They'll only care once they see us, and by then it'll be too late. Even if they stop us, it'll have to be at one of the stations," Victoria explained. "And the fun thing is that it's a civilian rail. Its next stop *is in the sector,* Joseph."

Max sighed. "How will the sector react?"

"I don't know. Can't precisely give them a call and find out. But we don't exactly look like security, you know."

Victoria traced the rail line with her finger. "It should terminate a few floors down," she said. "I don't think it would be connected to the main elevator system—too much traffic for that. Probably has its own personal one that ..."

As Joseph and Max trailed behind her, he put an arm on their shoulder. For balance, he said. They helped prop him up a little. He was moving in staccato, taking a few steps and resting, putting his hand on their shoulder and taking it away.

"What did you even shove in me?" He asked. "It feels like a goddamn dowel."

"I don't know," Max sighed. "I was just told to help, and it looks like it worked. Stopped the bleeding. When we get back and you can see a doctor, I'm sure it'll be better."

"Yeah, no, I won't be feeling better for months. Hell, if ever. I keep looking to the future and I keep seeing a jail cell. I keep seeing Earth, from the view of a courthouse window. What did we even *do*, Max?"

"We restored the Solarnet," they replied. "We went and we did what we were asked to do, what we wanted to do, and we're going home now. I don't know what else you want me to say there."

He grunted a little as he stepped down a few stairs, moving his hands to grip the railing as best he could. Victoria was looking behind her, at them, from the bottom. She was looking up at them with a smile, strained but not fake. Max could tell that much, at least.

"I don't know. I got everything I wanted out of this. Could do without the bullet, but we fucked up Ashe's plans. We helped everyone out, I guess."

"You're exhausted, Joseph," Victoria offered. "Don't worry about it too much."

He opened his mouth, about to say something more, and then nodded, walking down the stairs in silence. It was three flights of stairs, made of concrete and polished into a shine. Both Max and Victoria watched him carefully, ready to step in. He made it to the bottom, though.

The rail line had a train in it, only seven squat cars long, and locked in place. Inside were benches with individual partitions, metal armrests and rounded seats. After a moment of inspection, Max nodded over to Victoria.

"Any plan?"

"It can't be that hard to get in," Max said. "Let's just hop on and see what the driver's car has to offer."

Getting inside the driver's car was another matter. The train wouldn't let them on without a ticket or some sort of worker's authorization, of which they had neither.

Smashing the window and pulling the safety release latch from the inside wasn't particularly difficult. For all the fancy techniques and sly trickery one could do, brute force was often the best. The alarm sounded throughout the train station. The three of them looked at each other, their expressions all saying the same thing, tinged with exhaustion and pain. *Oh, fucking hell.*

They all knew it was going to happen. They all knew they had blown their cover. At this point, though, it didn't fucking matter. Victoria rifled through the backpacks, whispering to herself about guns. *Get the train moving. That's all that matters now, Max.*

Their hands shook and their heart pounded too fast in their chest. Cold sweat beaded on their forehead. As they tried to jimmy open the front of the train, they thought about what they had heard. About heart attacks, aneurysms, panic attacks. A little anxious voice whispered to them, doomsaying as they tried to focus. If it wasn't the guards, it'd be some organ failing, some vein popping like an overstuffed sausage. *God-fucking-dammit, Max, focus.* Keeping their tools in their hands was impossible. Sweat, shaking, god, their head …

The lock broke and they tore the door open. Spilling into the front car of the train, they looked around for just a breath.

The front of the train wasn't really a car by itself—it was a small, stubby section that had been cleaved off the frontmost car and contained, at most, a seat, a screen and a computer. Vertigo washed over Max as they sat down in the driver's seat and got to work. They could see everything from here, looking down from the station. The Spire pillars, the cables, the wires, platforms with little people running around and little drones hovering above. The lights and screens flickered with changing advertisements, smearing between colors.

Their fingers squeaked on the screen as they opened up the train's computer system. Noise from outside. They didn't want to look. They couldn't fucking look. Stare at the screen, try to make sense of it. Words swam, didn't register. There was no security, there was no obstacle. Perhaps it was an extra feature they didn't want to pay for, perhaps they relied on rough men who stood ready to protect business. *Sector A route.* Those words became clear, and Max tapped on the screen furiously, begging the train to respond.

When the train started to move, Max froze in place, their legs pressing together and their back pushing into the seat. They expected relief, to feel *good* about this, but they looked down at the ants moving around and their reactions. Rushing about, moving faster once they heard the train start, Max knew they were rushing to try and stop them. They allowed themselves a look behind, at the train slowly pulling away from the station. A K9 and its handler had rushed through the doors and was screaming something behind them. But before the other guards came in, the train had already left, quietly humming along its rail.

A drone hovered upward from the ground, taking a parabolic arc as it flew. Like a deer facing a car, Max didn't move an inch. Maybe the train would outrun it, pick up speed as it descended down the rail. It moved along at a steady pace, not shifting or changing. The drone got closer.

It wasn't that they were afraid of having their image taken. That had happened hours ago, at least. It wasn't that they were afraid of being knocked down—you would need artillery to knock this train out of the sky. It was more primal than that, knowing that they were being chased, knowing that there were a bunch of people waiting to hurt them, to hurt everyone around them. And these people knew exactly where they were going.

The drone watched them for a few minutes, hovering alongside the train until they slipped by into the tunnels too narrow to follow. Max finally let themselves breathe.

They got up to sit with the others. Joseph was leaning back as best he could on the rigid seats, Victoria was leaning on the wall. She was fidgeting a lot, lacing her fingers together and cracking knuckles repeatedly, looking from side to side.

"It'll be about ten minutes until we're at the sector," Max said. "I saw on the nav console. We're almost out of this."

"Yeah, great," she said. "You saw that drone, right?"

"Of course I did. It's like Joseph said. There's no way they wouldn't know where we were coming from."

"Sure, I'm just thinking now. We get to the sector, report back, what? We gotta get the PFs together. I'm just thinking ... hell, they *shot* Joseph. With live ammunition—"

"I am beyond aware of that, Vic," Joseph scoffed.

"Yeah, and I'm saying that's a hell of an escalation. We need to talk to people about that, we need to make sure that the Solarnet stays up. How ... " Her fidgeting got worse, Max could see her shoulders tense and relax, her eyes becoming more frantic. "Fuck, I hate the end of ops, so much to—"

"I have the access code to the Solarnet functionality on my laptop. Don't worry. I can give the code to most people, there's a function in the settings of most computers here that'll give you admin access. We give the code to ten, twenty people and boom. Secure."

"So long as none of 'em are rats," Joseph interjected.

"So be careful," Max said.

The station approached. The train slowed down. The station leading into the sector was clean and prim, far fancier than they remembered the sector being. They realized that was because this was for guests, for special workers, for those who lived in the Spire and had a commute. Not for them.

A bunch of folks stood in the station. At the doors, Max could see benches and decorations hauled up, twisted into a barricade, lashed together with thick chains. A few people had gathered on the other side. Their intensity was almost fiery hot, peering into the train car. Max felt the urge to put their hands up slowly, carefully, to wait for someone else to make the first move.

Victoria stepped up and opened the door. Her hands were up in a lazy, halfhearted pose.

"We have a wounded person," she said. Her voice cut through the silence, the tension. Someone clambered over the barricade to help. Others started pulling it away to create a passage.

"Solarnet," Max asked one of the barricade folks. "Is it up now?"

"Yeah," they replied nonchalantly. "It's been up for a few hours. Why?"

Of course, they didn't know *why* they'd asked. Probably didn't recognize them or that they were a PF. Max let out a deep sigh of relief, though. Final, proper confirmation. It wasn't all for nothing. It wasn't all a waste of blood and sweat and tears and time. They fought back the urge to celebrate, to jump up or hug or shout, and just nodded at the person.

"Thank you for letting me know," they said. Victoria pushed them along, trailing just behind Joseph. He was leaning against someone, answering a few questions here and there about how he felt and how he was doing.

"Fine," said Joseph. "Just patch me up and don't make me sit around in a hospital bed forever."

He was assured that wasn't going to happen. Someone mentioned a clinic—there had to be enough people here who knew what they were doing to take care of Joseph. He was going to be okay and that put Max's mind at ease just a bit.

"So," said Victoria. "I'm going to see if any of the PFs can meet. Should be an hour, two at most? Joseph, I'm not going to force you for obvious reasons. But if you can ...?"

"I'll be there. Hell or high water. Gonna make sure I get *credit*." He smiled sardonically.

"Oh," Max sighed.

"I'd appreciate it if you came, Max. I can't tell the whole story without you—you know what you did; I don't."

Max thought longingly of their bed—the messy sheets and the lumpy mattress seemed inviting right now. Every bit of their body was drained, even moving their arms felt like a struggle, like *they* were a substance sloshing around in a skinsuit everyone called "Max." But Victoria's smile was warm. Her eyes were as tired as Max's.

"Okay," they said. "I'm getting coffee first. I don't think I will be able to stay upright if I don't."

Chapter Thirteen

Coffee was served in seemingly perpetual amounts in the central area of the sector. In barely a day ... two days? Max didn't really know what time it was at this moment; it felt like eternity was mere hours ago. Temporal quandaries aside, Max couldn't help but be impressed. Entire stores were opened up, tables and chairs laid out. People had cleared space around fountains and set to work creating impromptu gathering spots. A collective of artists had gotten to work, painting a vast red and black geometric design, hanging it high up and above the jumbotron. The fabric hung over the screens loosely, the light of a still-active loop of B-roll barely peeked through.

The lineup for coffee was pretty long, but it gave Max more time to breath in the atmosphere, to see what was happening. Someone was playing guitar on the edge of a fountain. Another was scrawling furiously at a table, surrounded by paper and pens. Jittery people talked quickly, their cups shaking in their hands, and some slept under the shade of artificial trees, taking a few moments before someone else inevitably gave them a little nudge and the two of them walked away. People smiled and laughed and showed each other things on laptop screens and phones.

Satisfaction filled Max, a warm and gentle feeling of joy. They had helped make this possible.

Finally, they were in front of the coffee machines. Industrial-scale drip brewers were brought out, with caulk and drywall dust staining the corners where they had once been mounted to a wall. It had all different options—coffee, tea, dark roast, caramel, cream, sugar—all sorts of things to upsell someone on. Dark roast, caramel, cream. Max wasn't paying, they could have *this* indulgence. The coffee dribbled out pathetically more than poured, but it smelled hot and caffeinated and that was enough.

Victoria for her part wasn't still; nor did she spend time taking in the atmosphere. A phone in one hand and standing off to the side of the person she'd borrowed it from, she made call after call. Each one was short, curt.

"Hello. It's Victoria. Meet me for mission post-briefing. Dockyards seem quiet enough. Bye."

An hour later, Max and Victoria were facing people Max didn't recognize, who looked at them with only a vague air of recognition. *Oh, that person Victoria brought on,* they imagined each person thinking in turn.

The dockyards were incredibly quiet. Quieter than Max had heard it, more still than they had experienced it in years. The plain concrete and steel, the smell of ozone and dust, all of it was still there, but they felt off-kilter. No one else was here. No one else was working. Not even the automatons or robots on autopilot. It was just them, Victoria, and everyone she could round up.

Explaining what happened was simple enough. Max watched the people as Victoria got into the story. How they responded, what they thought. A blonde woman leaning against the wall seemed unperturbed, watching with an intensity Max found uncomfortable, even creepy. Like she was perceiving everything, absorbing every iota of sense but not moving at all. Another, a man—Max thought they recognized them as James from before they'd set out—kept his eyes fixed on Max, nodding along as Victoria spoke. He offered an approving, firm smile when Victoria explained how Max figured out the cold boot hack. Again, a fluttery, warm feeling moved through them.

Victoria kept asking if Max had anything to include, comments, criticisms. If this was some sort of meeting or debrief or discussion of what happened, Max was terrible at it. Vague commentary here and there, rubbing the back of their neck and saying some, "Oh, it wasn't much."

"But Joseph," said James. "He's what worries me right now. Deadly force is an escalation."

"An escalation we were expecting," said the woman.

"I know," said Victoria. "We knew it was a good fifty-fifty chance that we'd get shot at. I don't know if it was some asshole who was taught 'shoot first' or some scared dollar-store security guard who got given a gun once the strike started. But it doesn't matter. We need to get the other PFs to get ready for war footing."

"No way we'd win that," said Joseph. "We can strike, we can sabotage shit, but what? You want us to print a bunch more guns and act like a whole army now?"

"No," Victoria said. "I want us to be ready for when the guards come back. For when our strike gets hit hard. There's only so long we can hold out like this, and getting the Solarnet up was an *excellent* start. But we're not done yet. We're nowhere near done yet. I'm not asking you guys to act specops, but it's not like we can relax. Next meeting, we can talk in more detail when everyone's around, but for now—"

"Victoria," Max interjected. "We all know how serious it is."

"We're with you," said Joseph. James followed up with one of his approving nods.

She paused for a moment.

"Alright. We'll talk about this more later. If anything happens to the Solarnet, talk to Max. They know what they're doing."

"I changed the access codes. Have it on my laptop. They might be able to figure it out, might not. But I made sure to keep the computer parts, so at least they'll need to slow down a *little* bit."

The conversation ended on an awkward, slow note, bleeding out on the dockyard floor until no one had the will to keep it going. Goodbyes were exchanged, and people left.

"I won't keep you," said Victoria. "But do you want to meet with me later? At the Screwdriver?"

"Oh," Max nodded instinctively. "Yeah, sure. I'll be a few hours, though."

The apartment wasn't welcoming at all. They opened the door, expecting some sort of relief, some sort of joy at seeing their place. It was cold and stagnant. They took off their hoodie and tossed it aside. They tried to get their mind off it, but there was unease gnawing at them. They didn't want to be alone. Not right now.

But there wasn't much of a choice in the matter, and the one attractive, beautiful thing in the apartment was their bed.

Sleep eluded them, though. They were exhausted, everything hurt, their eyelids felt like wet, falling cement. But they could not sleep. Relaxation was impossible, lying in bed was pain in and of itself. And so, they looked at the clock, seeing that two hours had passed. Two hours spent shifting, groaning, trying to get comfortable. Sisyphus would have given up by now, and so Max rolled out of bed and let their muscles scream for a bit. One thought had been reverberating in their mind. Joseph. Was he okay?

No, obviously fucking not. Despite his assurance that he'd make the meeting, he'd been carted off to some clinic to be treated. But he had to have been treated by now. It might ... no, it *was, it had to be* worth at least checking on him now. They slouched their way out of their apartment and toward the main hall, asked where the clinic was and slouched toward it. Someone, politely, asked them what was wrong. Max said nothing but nodded affirmatively and walked away.

The clinic itself was part of the station proper. Set up for industrial accidents, injuries, sicknesses, calling it a clinic was more a denotation of its scale than anything—no more than a few dozen beds, expanded with cots and sleeping bags for people whose injuries were more "wait it out" than "treat constantly." The person manning the front desk was prim, proper, wearing makeup and a very professional pantsuit. This day was like any other to them, and when Max asked if there was a Joseph around, the response was simple.

"Last name?"

"Uh ... Ricci, I think. Joseph Ricci. Came in with ... gunshot wounds."

"Oh," the reply was understated, polite. "Yes. Room one-four."

Joseph's room was shared by five other people. He looked the worse among them. Others had scrapes and bandages on their head or their arm in a sling or something else. He was laying on the bed, eyes open, pupils dilated and smile dopey. He seemed to recognize Max and shifted in bed when they walked up to him.

"Ff-fuck," he slurred. "Max, hey. I'm ... fuck, got me all up on morph—" his head flopped a little to the side. He took a deep breath and tried to recompose himself. It was a valiant effort but sweat covered his skin and his whole complexion seemed just a shade lighter. "Why're you here?"

"I wanted to check up on you," Max pulled the small, plastic chair at the side of Joseph's bed over to them and sat down. "I wanted to apologize."

"What for?" The painkillers (Max noted the patient information whiteboard beside Joseph did not say *not* morphine) had brought him down to a strange, relaxed state. Max couldn't remember seeing him like this, with or without an IV drip stuck in his arm. "Didn't do anything to me."

"Joseph, you got *shot*," their tone rising a little bit, disbelief staining their words. "You got shot because—"

"Nah, not your fault. Didn't have the gun. Got out of there. Good work. We did good." Each sentence slurred into the next. "I'm fucked up, but that happens. Expected that to happen. Apologies ain't a medicine, so don't know why you're giving me one. Next time—next time we bring shields or something. Ol' warrior shit, make it all guarded."

Max let out a joyless chuckle. The drugs really were getting to him. "Okay. Sounds good to me. So, there'll be a next time?"

"Don't see why not. Fucked up, got fucked around with, but strike's still goin'. Keep it goin.'" He took a deep, long breath. "I ain't dead yet. Whenever the corpos play their next move, I wanna be frontline. Means you gotta keep this shit going until I'm outta this bed."

Max's chest swelled for a moment. They smiled and nodded. "Stay off my ass next time and we have a deal. But where'd all that shit about stuff going wrong go?"

Joseph's eyes rolled up and stared at the ceiling for a few moments. "Never said it'd be right off the bat. Went wrong though, huh? I'm here. More right than wrong, though. Every day's a dice roll. Gotta keep the pressure up. Keep letting corpo fucks know we don't like this shit. I'm still bettin' on this ending with a lotta shit. But for me, the other option's worse. Make 'em fight for their shit. Make 'em scared to lose their shit. Make 'em know we're trying to take our shit back. Can't let go of ourselves just cuz it's easier."

Max nodded. They sighed. "Good to know you're—"

"Not fucking dead is what I am, and that's just great," he chuckled. "Now doncha have better things to do than talk to me?"

Max took a deep breath. "Victoria and I are meeting at the Screwdriver soon."

"Save me a beer, eh?"

Max got up, bracing themselves against the hospital bed. "Of course. Talk to you later, Joseph."

Chapter Fourteen

The Screwdriver hadn't changed much. Jackson was still there, cleaning glasses and slinging cocktails. He was smiling though—a rarity. Gerry Rigg was serving drinks, rolling around and asking *valued customers* to sit down or relax or order a drink. No bouncer was present, though. Given how many people Max recognized from the PF meetings—faces they had seen but names they'd never learned—it didn't look like they needed one.

Gerry came over and asked them what they wanted. Nothing complex, just a beer for now. Waiting for someone, you see. Gerry didn't understand socialization or even just waiting for someone. With only a few days into the strike, no one had even bothered to change out its phraseology yet. When the beer was brought out, it happily chirped that Max had received a 100-percent discount, bringing the total price to zero dollars and zero cents.

Beer wasn't Max's favorite thing, but that's why they chose it. Sipping slowly and waiting for Victoria to show up, Max reflected on everything that happened. God, their arm ached, right where they got grazed. It pulsed and hurt, and they felt it through the fabric of their shirt every so often. They thought to their mistakes—the caution around the first K9, the boldness around the next. The train they took to get back, the tunnels they wandered to get to the server room. Regret welled in them, but it didn't stay long. They did what they'd set out to do. No one ... no one had died. That's what mattered in the end, right? But they couldn't stop thinking about alternatives, branching realities in which they had done better and in which they had done worse.

"Hello, Max," Victoria said. They snapped to attention and waved Victoria over. She sat down, rolling her shoulder a bit.

"So," she continued. "Are you doing okay?"

Max thought for a moment. "No," they said. "No. I hurt all over. I'm tired as can be. I had to drag myself out of bed, and I just feel really, really bad. I don't know what you want me to say. I can't imagine feeling anything but awful."

"So, are you done?" She asked. Max cocked their head. "I mean," she continued, "are you going to step away from doing a PF thing? I remember when you and I first met, and you seemed uncertain. Shaky, really. If Joseph hadn't vouched for you, I would have thought you were an informant. A really bad one."

Max chuckled. "I was afraid of that. I don't know, though. I'm hurting, like, physically. I'm in a lot of pain. Whenever I have free time, I just think about everything I did wrong. I'm exhausted. But the Solarnet's up again. I don't know what people are using it for but that's still good, right?"

"Twenty-two thousand dollars just got transferred to strike funds in the last hour. A lot of it from people outside the Federation of Unions. That's legal fees, that's rent, that's so that no matter what happens, as many people as we can manage are going to be okay. And that's not even the half of it," she said. "We're talking with Luna and Mars and the other stations. Where they haven't started already, there's something in the works. So, yes, we did something good."

Max looked around for a moment at nothing in particular. "And those other strikes, then, how're they going? What's the news?"

"LMC stock has crashed," Victoria said. "They're down, well, I don't understand the stock market, but someone said Mr. Ashe has probably lost somewhere in the tune of eighty billion dollars in the last day or so. And we have the capacity to strike for weeks." She smirked as she added the last part. He was still a trillionaire, of course, and it didn't feel like much would change that, but that delightful feeling of schadenfreude was hard to deny. "Luna's shut down most of its outgoing traffic. Almost nothing from the stations are getting to Earth. Station Two's still fighting. That place is mostly an asteroid-mining hub and 'repurposed mining lasers' is a phrase I've seen thrown around."

"Jesus," Max said. "And the Federation's posted its demands?"

"Oh yes," Victoria said. "And it's got us all sorts of trouble. Being called luddites, anti-progress, good for nothing—saying we should be *grateful* that we get room and board and food and live up in the stars. Recognition of the Federation, debt forgiveness, a delay for automation. Though between you and me," she leaned in, "those are a bit watered down. If it was up to me, it'd be that we make sure LMC and its ilk are *destroyed*."

"A bit of a hard sell," they leaned back. "It's been two days, right?"

"Two and a half," Victoria said.

"And in that time, we secured a whole sector for ourselves, restored the Solarnet. I don't even know what the other PFs have been up to, but I'm sure it's important work. And now we're facing the very real chance that security will regroup, hit us hard, and with ..." they trailed off for a moment, then shook their head. "Point being: I don't know. I look at everything we did. I think about everything that happened, about what Joseph said to me. Rebelling because it's good to make Ashe's ilk know how much people don't like them, not because you're gonna win. I don't know if I agree with him, but it keeps rattling around in my head. He kept saying we'd never win, that this was just a way to lash out. That our job's to fail well, not succeed."

"Yeah, I've heard the same from him. Make sure the CEOs know we hate their guts, even if it doesn't go anywhere. It's interesting and I get where he's coming from. But I don't know, Max, I can't say the same. I'd go insane if I did everything thinking it was just going to fall apart."

"I want this to work out," Max bit the inside of their cheek, chewing nervously. "And I don't want Ashe to have the satisfaction of beating us. But I can't help but circle back. I keep thinking about all the things we did wrong. I keep thinking and re-thinking. I keep imagining worlds and scenarios where we could have done better. I still feel the weight of him falling on me, you know? I remember cowering in the corner when the K9s came around, doing nothing when they were there. It all weighs on me," they finished the beer and put it to the side of the table.

"But at the same time, I can't do nothing. I told you when we first met—I want to help. I want to make things a bit better. Keeping my head down and letting my nerves win out ... I can't do that. I can't. Even if I don't do big PF actions or whatever, I want to help, be available. Despite everything, the fear, the stress, the exhaustion, the pain, I can't imagine doing anything else."

Victoria looked down at the table, mechanical fingers tapping quietly. "I'm glad to hear that, Max. I think we'll need someone like you a lot. This is all only just beginning. No matter how it ends in a few weeks or months, this here is a beginning."

Sometime later, after idle conversation and friendly chit-chat, Max found themselves looking out of the windows near the Screwdriver, watching the stars. For everything that had happened in the last few days, Max was of two minds. Fear, terror, joy, excitement—everything was changing. Being told point blank, being reminded every single day that their life was going to end and automation would swoop in and they'd be forced to uproot everything just to pay off debt to the company, that anger and rage and horror seemed distant and ever-present at the same time. Like it happened a million years ago, supplanted by far worse offenses, but nothing was possible without it.

Some sixty million miles away from Earth, Max was staring out into the stars. And for the first time in a long, long time, they felt like they were doing something worthwhile.

Acknowledgments

Writing a book is kinda hard, you know. A lot of people see writing as an innately solitary activity, something that a single person does alone. This isn't true, and despite the many lonely nights where it was me and my glass of gin doing the work, I had the full backing of many people and was supported, encouraged and helped by countless others. This book, like every other book, like all things in this world, was a group effort.

First, my thanks to AK Press for taking a bet on a new, young writer. It means the world. And alongside them, I want to thank Sanina, my tireless and skilled editor, who caught plot holes, grammatical errors, weird phrasing and more. They helped guide me through this journey, from the first email to the launch party.

Next, I want to thank my beta-readers. M.J. Walker, whose clashing ideas and different perspective were invaluable. Alexis G., most sympathetic to my requests for knowledge of medicine and the various horrors that can befall the human body and eternally supportive of my efforts. Pebble, xyr lively political debates and disagreements always serving as a whetstone for my own beliefs and what I brought to this story. Ada "Shinoı" Mackiewicz, a longtime pillar in my life and the person who introduced me to anarchist thought. Matthew Zakharuk, a good friend and someone whose input has always been appreciated. All of you helped contribute to *Station Six*, all of you made this story possible and as good as it could be.

My family supported me throughout this journey, and since I don't want to dox myself I will keep their identities concealed. But thank you, to Mom and Dad who raised me, Auntie and Uncle with whom I lived, Grandma for fostering my interest in politics and history, and my brothers (so many brothers that naming them could be a chore) for always being down for a tussle.

And finally, I want to thank my friends. Mutuals on Twitter, longtime friends I haven't seen for years, people I only talk to rarely, comrades in my hometown and those I spend every day with. You all helped me, either in making my day brighter, advising me on the process or simply by shaping me earlier in my life. I love all of you, and this wonderful existence is the reason why I wrote this book, and people like you are why I firmly believe a better world is possible.

I exist because of you, because of my connections to you all, because nothing in this world is an individual act. Not this book, not the computer I wrote it on, not me as a person. I owe the world to a world of people.